Changing of the Guard Dog

Also by Lane Stone

Pet Palace Mysteries
Stay Calm and Collie On
Support Your Local Pug
Changing of the Guard Dog

Changing of the Guard Dog

A Pet Palace Mystery

Lane Stone

LYRICAL UNDERGROUND
Kensington Publishing Corp.
www.kensingtonbooks.com

LYRICAL UNDERGROUND BOOKS are published by

Kensington Publishing Corp.
119 West 40th Street
New York, NY 10018

All Kensington titles, imprints, and distributed lines are available at special quantity discounts for bulk purchases for sales promotion, premiums, fund-raising, educational, or institutional use.

Special book excerpts or customized printings can also be created to fit specific needs. For details, write or phone the office of the Kensington Sales Manager: Kensington Publishing Corp., 119 West 40th Street, New York, NY 10018. Attn. Sales Department. Phone: 1-800-221-2647.

Lyrical Underground and Lyrical Underground logo Reg. US Pat. & TM Off.

First Electronic Edition: May 2019
ISBN-13: 978-1-5161-0194-8 (ebook)
ISBN-10: 1-5161-0194-4 (ebook)

First Print Edition: May 2019
ISBN-13: 978-1-5161-0195-5
ISBN-10: 1-5161-0195-2

Printed in the United States of America

Dedicated to my parents, Sue and Patrick Stone

Chapter 1

"Drowned," John said, carefully letting go of the corpse's wrist and rising from kneeling over the body in the sand. The dead man was on his back, his lower legs still submerged.

"In a tuxedo?" I asked, taking my eyes off the stranger so tangibly here though he'd journeyed to somewhere else. I scanned the quiet strength of the water of the Delaware Bay, so different from the nearby wild Atlantic Ocean.

He had stated the obvious. The man *was* dead and his body had washed up on Lewes Beach. So, while his assessment was probably correct, my clothing question was more intriguing. I looked back down at the youngish man with shoulder-length blond hair, stylishly cut and subtly highlighted, and imagined someone who in life would have evoked words like *flair* and *worldly*. In a different time, would we have called him a bon vivant?

"I can't believe I let you talk me into coming without my phone." He looked at me, *I told you so* all over his face.

I raised an eyebrow. "You agreed we should leave them at my place."

He was smiling as he reached out to pull me close.

I pushed back. "Not in front of him," I said, pointing to the dead man at our feet. "Kindly remember you're the chief of police." We were having our first day of real spring and while the weather was warm enough for locals to come to the beach, as many had, it was not inviting enough for anyone to venture farther than Lewes Beach proper. That is, the main section of the beach near the parking lot. John and I had smugly jogged northwest up the strip of sand, away from the masses. Now we were paying for it.

He nodded and looked around. "It didn't do much good to separate you from your phone after all. How many people have we seen here that

Lane Stone

know you?" He was right. We'd seen my Buckingham Pet Palace assistant manager, Shelby Ryan, and her Bernese Mountain Dog, Bernice, and Kate Carter with her collie mix, Robber, along with several other pet parents. "Too bad no one's around now." He ran his hand over his short hair. The gesture was so familiar to me now. He was stalling. "I hate to ask, but will you go find someone with a phone and call the station? I'll stay with him."

"You're a much faster runner. Why don't I stay here? You know I've seen a dead body before. Two. I won't fall apart."

"I also know that both times you were more upset than you let on," he answered, putting a hand on my shoulder and massaging my bare skin with his thumb.

I looked at my watch and then at the jumble of footprints leading to and from the body. "I'm okay. Just hurry. It's almost ten o'clock. The first high tide will be at ten forty."

John tilted his head and asked, "How do you know that?"

"Just find someone with a phone," I said, instead of answering that beach people keep up with both the weather forecast and the tide tables, then I shooed him away.

"This is so wrong, even for Lewes, Delaware. I'm probably breaking every rule in the book." He was still grumbling as he turned and jogged back to the populated part of Lewes Beach. I watched his back and was again surprised at how quickly he moved for a man so muscular and tall. Then I turned back to stand guard over the dead man. I let myself be mesmerized by the water lapping against my feet; thinking that since we were on the bay rather than at, say Cape Henlopen, on the ocean side of Lewes, I didn't have to contend with the strong waves to keep the body where we found it.

A breeze blew through the beach grass on the dune separating the beach from the nearest homes. Only a line of rooftops in varying styles and a balcony here and there could be seen from where I stood and waited. I wondered if it would have made more sense for John to go to one of those houses, rather than back to the growing crowd of people, then remembered how few of them were occupied this time of year. He might have had to knock on several doors before finding anyone at home. It was early spring in what we called Lower, Slower Delaware, or LSD, and summer felt so far away.

I heard a high-pitched squeal and jerked my head away from the expensive homes to see a woman and a boy walking my way. She lurched along in her strappy espadrilles, and the kid wore knee-length shorts and a baseball cap so far back on his head that the bill pointed to the sky. I'm not a kid person and could only estimate his age. He was somewhere between six and twelve years old.

"Is that crab dead?" the child yelled, pointing at his sandaled feet.

I looked down and spoke to my charge. "Uh-oh. Be right back." Then I gave the woman a friendly wave and walked the twenty or so feet to meet them. "This section is closed." That was kind of true.

The woman raised her designer sunglasses onto her head and twisted her outlined, plumped-up lips. "This is a public beach! There are no closed sections," she hissed.

I looked over her shoulder, down the beach to see if John was returning. No such luck.

"I want to find more dead crabs!" the kid wailed. If he didn't go back the way he'd come he was going to see something dead other than a crustacean.

"I'm sorry," I began. To think that seconds before I was concerned the kid would be traumatized seeing the body; now all I cared about was protecting the crime scene and the dead man's right to a little privacy and dignity. "This area is closed for now."

The kid was pointing past me and yelling, "Then why does he get to stay?"

"Nice try," I said. I was only slightly aware of movement on the berm as I turned my head. Then I saw the brat wasn't kidding. A man was hunched over the body and rummaging through his tuxedo pants pockets. "Stop!" I yelled.

"She's crazy, Mom. Let's go!" the kid said.

I took off running the short distance back to the man who had been left in my care, yelling as I sprinted, "Get away from him!"

The thief looked up but didn't stop scrounging through the dead man's pockets. He reached across the torso to the pocket on the other pant leg. His hands moved quickly and with determination, but the slack expression on his face was *lights are on but nobody's home*. I charged him and launched myself into the air to shove him away from the body.

Somewhere in midflight, time slowed down. I was aware that although the thief was looking in my general direction, he wasn't looking at me. Suddenly I felt myself being lifted, and as time sped up I was thrown down face-first onto the sand. While I was still wondering what in the hell was going on, a hand shoved the back of my head, holding my face under water. A knee was pressed into the small of my back, and with his other hand he pinned my right arm against my back. I struggled and fought and turned my head to the right, toward the crowd and hopefully to John. I lifted my head just an inch, but that was enough to gulp some air. He tried to yank my hair, but it was too short to grab and so he pushed me back underwater, grinding my cheeks into the small shells and pebbles. I kicked into the sand, ineffectual but I had nothing to lose. Suddenly my brain was tracking details. Like the way his fingers had stretched wide as his palm pushed down on my skull. I arched my back and pushed up with my left hand, twisting my head to the left. "Help!" I screamed when my mouth was above the water.

My attacker let go of my right arm but kept the weight of his knee on my back. I could see the man who had been going through the victim's pockets. The expression on his face metamorphosized from a stupid blank to hurt confusion and finally to terror. I heard a noise that sounded like a bang. Once. Twice. As I watched, a dot of red appeared on the T-shirt he wore, then another, then they grew. He looked down at his shirt with a baffled expression on his face, then collapsed onto the dead man in the tuxedo.

"No!" I yelled.

Then my face was back under water.

"Bitch!" the man yelled, and I realized I hadn't known my assailant was a man until then. That had been my assumption because of his strength, but until I heard his voice, it had been a guess.

I felt the movement of water next to my right ear and opened my eyes a slit, and immediately felt the sting from the saltwater. I caught a glimpse of his hand, underwater and holding the gun. I saw his thumb sinking into the sandy bottom. I saw the barrel, longer than I thought it would be, and his palm wrapped around the handle, and his wrist. Was he about to shoot me in the face?

Suddenly he pushed down on my face with much more force and determination. I felt my cheek being pierced over and over. How naive I'd been. I had actually thought that he'd only been trying to keep me down. Too much an idiot not to follow that to its logical conclusion. He intended to kill me. I never thought I would die in the ocean. My lungs had stopped hurting. I let my eyes close. All I had to do was let myself drift away.

No! I thrashed and arched my neck and upper back. Now I was in survival mode. I kicked my legs and feet again and tried for purchase in the sand. Suddenly his knee came off my spine. Then his left hand came off the back of my head and his right hand jerked out of the water.

I became aware of the sound of dogs barking as I rolled over and pushed myself to a sitting position, ignoring how my eyes stung from the salt water. I sputtered and coughed and tried to stand, but my legs weren't ready for that. Then I shook my head in an attempt to clear my vision. Bernice and Robber were running away. No, they were chasing someone.

The man roared and ran for his life. He slowed, reached around and fired his gun in the direction of the dogs. The shot went wild since he hadn't aimed. That would have scared any sane human from continuing the chase, but not dogs. The unfamiliar sound probably confused them, but they ran as fast as the soft sand would allow.

He was running again and still I hadn't seen his face. That last attempt to kill had happened so fast, and the thought that one of those majestic dogs might be lying lifeless was so shocking, that I had recoiled in horror, something I would regret later.

I had known both Bernice and Robber since they were puppies, but even if I had my wits about me, I could not have predicted whether or not they would bite a person who was running *away* from them. Neither had been trained as guard dogs. The tone of the barking wasn't particularly alarming, but he didn't need to know that.

Then there was a man running into the sand dune through stalks of Cape American Beach Grass behind my attacker and the two dogs, and he was a different story. Chief John Turner *was* trained to attack.

All four had blown by the "KEEP OFF THE DUNES AND BEACH GRASS" sign. They tromped on the beach grass, which had thick but brittle stalks easily broken just by walking through one of these areas. For the first time in my life, I was glad to see someone disturbing the dunes.

Chapter 2

"Sue! Are you hurt? Do you think you can stand up?" Shelby yelled. She and Kate Carter reached me at the same time. Still greedily gulping air, I pulled my eyes away from the opening in the dune to look at them.

Kate jerked to a stop when she saw the two dead men. Blood from the chest of the man my assailant had shot was flowing into the water. I let Shelby help me to my feet. In an attempt to look "fine, just fine," I may have bounced upright too quickly. Anyway, I was lightheaded. I bent over and rested my hands on my knees. Now that I had the precious air I needed, the stinging from the salt water was back with a vengeance. I rubbed my eyes with the back of my hand, which only made it worse.

I figured I could try to make sense of all that had happened later, but for now I wanted to see John and the two dogs come back to the beach and know they were all right.

"There's the police," Shelby said, still holding my elbow. She was in her late forties but never seemed to age. She had long, thick, curly red hair, and I often told her I suspected she was actually a Chia Pet. Though she was barely five feet tall, she was strong and had no trouble supporting me.

The two officers were far away and looking around. Kate waved her arms over her head. "Over here!" she yelled.

When they were closer I recognized Officer Statler and nodded at her.

"Good to see you…" Her voice died away when she saw my face. I realized both cheeks stung, and when I gave each a swipe, grit and pebbles fell away.

A rustling to the side announced the return of the two dogs. Bernice and Robber gamboled through the opening in the sand dune and bounded up to their pet parents. I straightened to hug and thank them.

"Sue!" It was John, and he ran to me.

"Are you okay?" He tried to pull me close, but I reached my arm out, elbow locked, blocking him.

Without taking his eyes off my face, he reached for my closed fist and turned it palm up. With his other hand, he pried my fingers open. "What's this?"

I let him take the thumb drive. "It was in his pocket," I said. "I guess the water was churning so much that it floated out." I shrugged. "So I grabbed it."

John took it from me with two fingers and gently lowered my arm and hugged me. "I couldn't get to you in time," he said into the side of my wet, salty, sandy head.

"The dogs did," I said.

"Noted."

To say he's not a dog person would be the understatement of all time, so I was happy for this credit-where-credit's-due concession.

I pulled back and looked around his shoulders to the dunes. "He got away?"

"Someone pulled up in a car and he jumped in. I got a partial license—" Suddenly his hands fell away from my back. "Wait, didn't I leave you here with just one dead body?"

He walked around me and handed the USB drive to Officer Statler, then said, "Take a few photos." He was back in Chief Turner mode. He looked out at the distance, then down to where the water met the sand. "Then we'll pull the body back if we need to. Guess that's the best we can do while we wait for the crime scene team." I followed his gaze to the "weird perimeter," so-called because the line where the beach ended could symbolize anything or be nothing. I was listening to John, but I was disappearing, too.

A breeze came off the water and I shivered. I gave them a quick account of how while I'd been yelling at one man to leave the dead man alone, someone else had come from nowhere and tried to drown me. "I never saw his face, just his hand."

John and Officer Statler had a few more questions for me. I remembered the impression of movement in the beach grass and told them about that.

"Whose pocket is this from?" Officer Statler asked.

"Tuxedo man," I said, jerking my head in the direction of the original victim.

"Did you hear the one that attacked you say anything to his partner?" John asked, pointing to the carnage on the sand. "Or did the other man say anything?"

"No," I said, looking down at the second victim. His lank hair was light brown. The sides and back were cut short, and the top was longer. "You think they were partners?" The man who had been shot was around the age of the drowned man, but the similarities stopped there. Whereas the first victim had seemed robust, he was wiry and pasty. "If that was a *partnership*, it was past its sell-by date." I spoke slowly, trying to get clear on why I thought that.

"Not what I would call a good working relationship," Shelby said.

I bit my lip hard and managed not to cry. For every person who tries to kill you, there's a friend who knows just what to say. I didn't want sentimentality or drama. Her little joke had been perfect.

I cleared my throat. "I got the impression they knew one another." I thought about the way the second victim had looked at the man who, mere minutes later, was to be his killer. Maybe, just maybe, his dim expression had been fawning.

"It seems the man who fled was holding you down to give victim two time to go through victim one's pockets, probably looking for that thumb drive—but you're right, we don't know their relationship yet." As John spoke, he occasionally patted his own pockets. He was looking for his trusty notepad. How many other idiosyncrasies did we track on each other? We had been officially dating since the last murder in our little beach town of Lewes.

"Wouldn't it have made more sense to shoot *me*?" I asked.

"Kind of," Shelby offered.

Everyone looked at her.

"Shelby!" Kate said.

"Sorry," she apologized.

I moved over to hug her. "Ah, it's okay. He *was* trying to drown me, so it's not like he had a problem resorting to violence." I laughed and shook my head. That was when I glanced at Bernice and Robber and noticed how the two dogs were behaving.

It's not in a dog's nature to act sneaky, but both Bernice and Robber bobbed their heads rather than keeping eye contact. They moved close, then backed away. "Hey, you two," I said, going to stand in front of them. I reached under the Bernese Mountain Dog's chin and lifted it to see her face better. "Drop it." She opened her massive jaws and a cell phone fell out onto the sand. I looked over at Officer Statler, knowing John wouldn't want this job, and she already had a plastic bag out of her pocket. She reached down and scooped the phone into it.

"Hmm, whose phone is that?" John asked. He was still looking at me, but I think talking mostly to himself.

"It could belong to either of the dead men or to the guy who ran away," Shelby said.

Now it was the collie's turn. "Robber, do you have anything for me?" I asked.

Who? Me?

I knew Kate's dog well enough to reach for her mouth. She automatically opened up and I pulled the strip of fabric off her fanglike canine teeth, or cuspids. Officer Statler had another bag at the ready and I put the navy cloth in it.

"Kate, you didn't give him a command to do this, did you?" I asked, though I knew the answer. "To chase the man and attack him?"

"No, I don't know what that would be." Dogs have a drive to protect, and their inherent aggression has to be channeled. At Buckingham's we do that by training pet parents to be the leader of the pack.

The image of my attacker firing his gun at the dogs flashed in front of my eyes and I cringed.

"Sue," John said. "I think you should go to the hospital to be checked out."

"Exactly how bad do I look?" I asked. He didn't answer, which told me either I really looked beat up or he was thinking about everything he needed to be doing thanks to not one but two dead men on Lewes Beach.

"Okay," I said. "Can someone give me a—"

"You'll go?" John asked, astonished. His attention was off his to-do list, and he leaned closer to look into my eyes. "I mean, just like that?"

"Sure," I said.

"What's going on in that head?" Then he looked at the dogs. "You're going to ask if anyone has come in to be treated for a dog bite, aren't you?"

"Maybe." Obviously, I was no better at keeping secrets than the dogs were.

"I'll go with her," Shelby said. "Kate, would you take Bernice to Buckingham's? Lady Anthea and Dana are there."

Kate agreed, and took Robber's leash from around her shoulders and hooked him up. Then she did the same with the leash Shelby handed her. I watched as she retraced her steps down the beach to the parking lot, both dogs ambling alongside her, not a care in the world.

I turned to John. "So, we have two murders to solve."

"Wrong on both counts. There's no *we*." He pointed to the man in the tuxedo. "And this one could have been an accidental drowning."

I shook my head. "They were both murdered."

John shook his head, too. "Could be somebody helped him drown, but I don't want to turn him over just yet to see."

Officer Statler interrupted us. "The cavalry's here." She motioned to the opening in the berm and we saw the crime scene techs and medical examiner's office investigators, who would perform scene investigation, filing through.

I had to talk fast. "Are you saying the second victim just showed up here? *And* his killer? It's too much of a coincidence to think the guy just washed up where he could be found, since where a body washes up is pretty unpredictable." I swung my arm in an arc. "Everything is wrong about this."

"He could have been going for the guy's wallet or his watch," John said.

I didn't answer. His scenario didn't feel right, but I wasn't clear on why I couldn't buy it. All I knew for sure was that my attacker was out there somewhere, and as long as he was, there would be a finger on the trigger of a gun and a knee on my back and a hand holding my head under water.

Chapter 3

I checked the time on the computer monitor and groaned to Shelby and Dana. "I thought they only needed the room for three hours. They've been in there over four." Last month during an episode of community spirit and temporary insanity, I'd agreed to let a senior citizens' group use one of our rooms for a few hours to hold a driving skills refresher class.

Shelby shrugged. "I'm surprised Charles Andrews is putting up with it, even if it does get him a discount on his car insurance."

I groaned. She was talking about one of the oldest citizens in Lewes, and the most cantankerous. "I bet Lady Anthea is regretting signing up for the class," I said. "I'm surprised she hasn't bolted."

"Why did she want to waste her time on an American driver's ed class anyway?" Dana asked. She wore black leggings, a white oxford shirt with our logo, and hiking boots, along with a green Buckingham's sweatshirt tied around her narrow waist. She, like Mason, our lead groomer and one of the best on the Delaware coast, used fashion to communicate.

"She thinks it'll help her learn to drive over here," I answered. "If she starts coming over more often she'll want to be more independent."

I rubbed my cheek. It still burned from the abrasion and I pictured grains of sand hiding in my skin, though I'd been assured by Shelby and Dana that wasn't the case. All that was on my skin was skin. Every time I closed my eyes I felt I was back under water. I couldn't stop replaying the attack in my head. "The conductor for the Potomac Symphony Orchestra retired and it was a big deal to see him at his last concert. She had already scheduled her yearly visit for that, so the timing worked out for the class. Or at least that was the plan."

"I saw that in the newspaper," Shelby said. "His name is Daniel Laurent. Was she disappointed when he backed out and they assigned a mystery conductor to us?"

"No, she has the inside scoop on who the mystery conductor is and she's thrilled. This guy sounds like the Elvis of classical music," I said. "He's also a *composer* and she said he's going to debut his latest right here in Lewes this week. She said hearing it was on her music bucket list."

"A music bucket list?" Shelby asked. "Like hearing Jimmy Buffet in Key West?"

"Yeah, or going to Graceland," I answered.

"Or the Spice Girls reuniting and singing at a royal wedding," Dana added. "But still, she came to see a famous conductor and we have another murder. Plus, she's stuck in a class with an almost-ninety-year-old woman who doesn't know when enough is enough." She looked at her high-tech watch. "Ugh."

"Maybe they're wrapping up." Choosing to ignore their skepticism, I slid off the stool and walked down the hall to the playroom ordinarily reserved for puppies. I listened in and heard Charles Andrews shout to someone, "Oh, grow a pair!" He had a rather singular command of the English vernacular for a man in his eighties and he was not afraid to use it, but I had never heard him use that language in front of So-Lo and So-Long, his Dachshunds. He had insisted on bringing the dogs. They were probably a distraction because they're so cute, but since this was, after all, Buckingham *Pet Palace* we could hardly tell him no. Not that he had asked for our okay.

I opened the door enough to lean in and scan the room to see who he was talking to. The instructor was a woman about Mr. Andrews's age. Her white hair was pulled into a neat bun and what makeup she wore had been expertly applied, though with a rather heavy hand. She had partnered a wine-colored pantsuit with berry lipstick, indicating effort and maybe even a little cunning. How had she taken his outburst?

Charles was staring down a couple of younger men. They were probably in their fifties, mere pups compared to the others in the class. One wore round metal-frame eyeglasses and his friend sported facial hair that was either a neatly trimmed beard or stubble. I couldn't make the distinction from where I stood. Charles Andrews wasn't done. "If you have something to say, say it. You're adults, for Pete's sake! Put your hands down!"

One then the other looked to the instructor for her support, or perhaps protection. She ignored them, keeping her eyes glued to Mr. Andrews. The younger men exchanged looks with one another, and by consensus, slowly lowered their raised hands. "We were just waiting to be called on," one said.

I was dying to get Lady Anthea's take on the exchange but all I could see was the back of her head. We'd debrief tonight over drinks.

The instructor smiled at Charles Andrews and, I swear, batted her mascaraed eyelashes. I couldn't stomach any more of what looked like fawning over the crankiest man in town and went back to the calm of the reception desk.

"Symphony orchestra!" I yelled. Dana and Shelby turned and stared at me. "The murdered guy in the tux! He's got to be in the symphony!"

Dana jumped up from her stool and pointed a finger at me. "Legitimate," she declared. Then she angled the laptop on the desk to reach it better and started typing.

"Thanks," I answered. "I kept trying to think of a restaurant in Lewes where the waitstaff wears a tux, but we're not that kind of town."

"Yeah," Shelby agreed. "That's too far even for Rehoboth Beach." Her cell phone pinged and she read the text message. "This is from Mason. He wants to know what's going on with the investigation."

"How does he know about the body, I mean bodies? Shelby, did you tell him?" She shook her head.

"Is it on the internet already?"

Same negative response from Shelby.

Then I saw that Dana had lowered her head a few inches and was typing even faster, causing her natural hair to sway.

"Daaaana?" I called.

Before I could say more, the two sets of double doors opened and Chief Turner came in, now wearing his uniform.

"I may have mentioned it to Mason and Joey," Dana said, sheepishly. "I love that Bernice and Robber saved you."

I shook my head in mock exasperation.

"So do I," John said with a slow grin. "Sue, how are you feeling?"

"Fine." I even shrugged a shoulder to reinforce my it-was-no-big-deal, whopper-lie version of how I really was.

"Mason says his friend at the hospital reported in and *still no dog bite patients*," Shelby said, reading from her phone.

"Did he say what he was wearing?" Dana asked, to which Shelby shook her head no.

"Thanks," I said. "Tell him to keep up the good work."

John was pinching the bridge of his nose and shaking his head.

"Isn't this where you say we're not to get involved?" I asked.

"This isn't like the last time when you found yourselves in the middle of a murder investigation." He was back in full-metal Chief Turner mode, addressing the three of us.

"The last two times," Dana corrected him.

"Whatever," he said. When he spoke again, his words were clipped. "What happened on the beach this morning was *professional* and not at all like the others. We don't have much information on the first victim yet, but what you witnessed was murder in cold blood, and it has me worried." He shook his head and exhaled, like he was trying to get control of a mental image. "Anyway, I just dropped by to be sure Beebe Hospital gave you a clean bill of health."

I gave my tablet a jiggle to wake it up and nodded, feeling John's eyes inspecting my face.

"Were you able to read the USB drive?" Shelby asked.

John turned his gaze to her. He had progressed from suspicious to certain, all because of the way she'd hopped to a new topic of conversation. "Crime lab has it," he answered. "Sue, you did go to the hospital, didn't you?"

"Oh, yes!"

"What did the doctor say?"

"I didn't exactly see a doctor."

"So, what did the nurse say?"

"I wouldn't say I saw a nurse."

"Who looked you over then?"

"The guys in valet parking," Shelby said, laughing out loud.

Dana gave her a high five and then leaned over to me. "Niiiiice."

"They're high school kids!" John yelled.

"They're seniors in high school," Dana explained.

He rolled his eyes to show he was still not impressed, even with the addition of this new credential.

"Most of them are football players," she added.

"Well, with detective credentials like that around town, I'm thinking I better dust off *my* resume," he said.

Dana and Shelby laughed and I did, too. "Think about it," I said. "They see *everyone* coming in or leaving. A doctor or nurse would only be able to tell me about their own patients."

He pulled his cell phone out of his pocket. "I'll send someone over to talk to them."

"No need. Mason and Joey are on it," Dana assured him.

He rolled his eyes. "I want that parking lot scanned for the car that picked up the shooter. I should have thought of that first thing." He walked away to call his dispatcher, then came back to the desk. "So, what did the guys in valet parking have to say?"

"No dog bites today," I said. "To make it up to you, I think I know something about the first victim. We think he was in the symphony orchestra that's performing in Lewes this weekend."

Before he could praise me for cracking the case wide open, the doors to the puppy playroom were flung open with such force they hit the golf course-green hall walls. So many feet were stampeding toward the lobby that it sounded like Pamplona's running of the bulls. Dana, Shelby and I were protected by the desk. Chief Turner jumped back. Only a fool would have stood still. A parade of about twenty or thirty men and women stormed from the hallway into the lobby, passing us without saying goodbye, headed for the front door. They looked like supercompetitive racewalkers pumping their arms, bent at ninety degrees. Some took quick looks back, aware of the fact that they didn't have to be first out, but they'd better not be last. The fact that Buckingham's has inner and outer doors before you can exit created a bottleneck, backing up the lobby with angry citizens.

The two men Charles Andrews had yelled at were in the middle of the throng, scowling and huffing.

"I cannot believe the nerve of that man!" one fumed.

"Neither can I!" his friend replied.

Shelby, Dana and I exchanged glances.

"We're right there with you," Dana muttered. Every time Charles Andrews brought So-Long in for day camp there was some fresh abuse to be tolerated. So-Lo, a senior dog, usually stayed home, but was here today.

Next came the two Dachshunds, sprinting on their short little legs. That surprised me because Mr. Andrews rarely let them out of his sight, since he believed no one knew anything about dog care other than himself. Had he told the two dogs to run ahead and save themselves? The mystery was swiftly solved, though, when he followed them, not speaking but silently shooing them with his two hands.

The instructor ran up the hallway, waving a stack of papers over her head. "Your certificates!" she yelled.

"Keep 'em," someone in the group growled over his shoulder.

The room had cleared except for a few stragglers, including the two men Charles had told to "grow a pair," who had stepped aside. "Should we go back and get them so we are eligible for the discount?" He was either new to town or a weekender. I didn't know him. He wore corduroy pants and a plaid flannel shirt. Seemingly of their own accord, my eyes went to his hands. They were thrust into his pockets.

"Hell, no," his friend answered. "We just had to make an appearance." I ran my eyes down the arms of his cashmere turtleneck sweater. Before I could check out his hands, he'd turned and collided with Charles Andrews.

Andrews wheeled around. "Watch out for the dogs!"

The more expensively dressed man thrust his face forward. "Look here, old man...."

The two glared at each other. My overtaxed brain tried to make sense of the scene playing out a few feet away from me but it stalled out. How could he or anyone speak to a man of Charles Andrews's advanced age like that? The two Dachshunds sensed something wasn't right and backtracked. The high-pitched barking started before they had come to a full stop.

John moved forward. "I better get out there."

"What's your hurry?" Shelby whispered, making Dana giggle.

"Those dogs had better not go for my ankles," he said.

While it was true that every encounter with Mr. Andrews was unpleasant, I didn't like what I'd seen and didn't want that kind of animosity in the middle of Buckingham's lobby. Not today.

John slid in between the scowling men and growling dogs without looking at any of them. They had no choice but to move along. As he stood there his phone rang and he nonchalantly took the call. When the miscreants were out the door he walked back to the reception desk. "It should be down by Monday afternoon," he told the caller and hung up. "Just somebody complaining about the crime scene tape on the beach. She wants to hold a press conference and finds it unsightly." The curl of his upper lip told me what he thought of the caller's word choice. "I wanted to tell her I was sorry someone inconvenienced her by getting himself murdered." He shook his head.

"Charles Andrews probably would've said worse than that," Dana said.

I looked down the hallway. The teacher hadn't been last out of the puppy room. "We're missing someone. Lady Anthea?" I called. I didn't get a response, so I left the footdraggers in the lobby and went to the puppy room. My nose detected a top note of floor cleaner, then the odor of eau de puppy. I couldn't help but smile.

She was calmly folding the rented chairs and placing them on the trolley we'd been provided.

"What happened? Why did everybody run out like that?" I asked.

"It seems she mentioned her great-grandchildren one too many times and there was a rebellion." I stared at her as she walked to the table where snacks and drinks had been left out.

"Are you all right, Lady Anthea?"

She turned back to me and gave me a weak smile. "Of course, why do you ask?"

"You seem, well, not yourself." Had the occasional Lewes craziness finally worn her down?

"Oh, I'm fine." I knew what it meant when I gave that answer and decided to ask again later.

"Well, I have a bit of news," a baritone voice behind me said. "Sue, you're right about the first victim, the one in the tuxedo; he was with the symphony orchestra. His name was Georg Nielsen."

"Are there two Georg Nielsens?" Lady Anthea asked, then answered her own question. "I guess there could be many. The famous Georg Nielsen certainly isn't dead."

"The victim was a composer and a sometime symphony conductor," John said.

Lady Anthea's head jerked back. "No, no. He's too, well, *alive* to be dead. I mean, he's young."

John and I slowly nodded our heads. "The victim was young," he said. His tone was gentle, but not patronizing.

"And Georg Nielsen is a genius, a prodigy," Lady Anthea continued.

I shrugged. Having met him, you might say, late in life, I had no idea what his IQ was. John and I stood and waited. She'd get there when she was able. When she was ready.

Lady Anthea raised one eyebrow. "The musical world cannot possibly be without Georg Nielsen!"

Chapter 4

Lady Anthea and I finished straightening the room to get it ready for its usual occupants, four-legged and twice as civilized as today's, who would begin arriving at seven o'clock Monday morning. She looked around the room and smiled. The walls were painted burgundy and, as in all our rooms, we had decorated with a few pieces of dark wood furniture. Two rocking chairs and a table sat at the far end of the room. Bins of training aids and water bowls were placed along the walls. The floor was washable for practicality.

When we went back to the lobby, Dana had gone home. In the morning she'd return to her campus in Manhattan. She was a freshman at City College of New York. She'd chosen that school so she could continue to model.

John had gone, saying he'd see me later. He promised he'd let us know the identity of the second victim when he learned it.

"Damn," I said before noticing that Shelby was on the phone. I turned to Lady Anthea and lowered my voice to a whisper. "I forgot to ask him about the cell phone we got from Bernice's mouth." The lapse made me feel like I was slipping, but I consoled myself with the thought that the attack had happened only hours ago. Mental images were popping up at strange times but were never far away. Like when I looked at the water dispenser and thought about how we'd argued over flavoring it with coconut water—Shelby and me—or strawberries and basil—Mason and Joey. We had settled on the latter since it seemed more British. Now it seemed not only unimportant, but downright silly. Was it normal to divide my life between before and after, the way I was doing? Surely not.

Shelby was giving her caller our email address, so it must not be one of our current pet parents. She rolled her eyes and hung up. "I can't believe that," she said with a grimace. "She's staying with someone and didn't ask in advance if she could bring her dog. Who does that?"

"I've never heard of such a thing," Lady Anthea said with a huff.

"If she's calling us on a Sunday, I guess her friends told her no," I said.

Shelby nodded. "She's already filled out the online registration form. Her vet is in Washington, DC and she'll have the dog's medical records sent to us."

"What breed?" Lady Anthea said.

"Pekingese. And her name is Cordy Galligan. She'll be here tomorrow—"

"Cordy Galligan!" Lady Anthea cried.

Shelby nodded. "Yeah. Do you know her?"

Lady Anthea clapped her hands. "Cordy Galligan's dog is coming to Buckingham Pet Palace!"

"Uh, yeah. Assuming the dog passes the temperament evaluation," I said. I had no idea who this Cordy person was but the mention of her name had brightened my business partner's mood considerably.

"Should we know who that is?" Shelby rested her elbows on the counter, all ears.

"She's the concertmaster of the Potomac Symphony Orchestra!" She looked up at the ceiling. "Hopefully this town won't kill her, too."

"Ouch," I said.

"I'm sorry," Lady Anthea said, patting my shoulder. "I'm just so terribly relieved you weren't seriously hurt, or worse, this morning. When Kate Carter came in with the two dogs and told us what had happened, we couldn't believe what we were hearing. Then we learned that Georg Nielsen was dead. And you must admit we've had our share of—" Lady Anthea stopped talking and stared straight ahead. "Oh, noooo."

"What is it?" Shelby asked.

"My brother."

"He's coming tomorrow. We know," I said.

"I didn't exactly tell him about the last murder. I couldn't after his reaction to my very slight involvement in the investigation into Henry Cannon's death."

"Uh, let me stop you there," I said. "Very slight involvement? We were almost killed solving it."

She raised her hand in a stop signal, and nodded in agreement. "I hate to ask, but would you not mention the last one to him?"

"No problem," I said. I remembered how annoyed he'd been when he saw the family name on Google Alerts and demanded that Lady Anthea come back to England. He was worried that the royal family would be told about it. Their grandmother had been lady-in-waiting to the queen, meaning their lives were governed by a different set of rules than mine, assuming I had any.

"I won't say a word," Shelby assured her, "but what about the rest of the town? Are you hoping gossip about Georg Nielsen will knock it off the rumor mill?"

"I'm hoping for more than that," she answered.

"You want to keep news of *this* murder, I mean these *murders,* from him?" I ventured.

She nodded, and Shelby and I stared in disbelief. "He never reads a newspaper and I'm the only person he knows here. I doubt he'll meet anyone other than those of us at Buckingham's."

I didn't dare look at Shelby, my partner in google-stalking Lady Anthea's brother, the duke. There seemed to be no limit to his snobbishness. He was pompous and conceited, and he was as dumb as an overbred brick. Tricking someone who was too proud to speak to the lowly citizens and too dumb to catch on if he overheard anything about the two dead men was like the opposite of a perfect storm. Everything was in our favor. As Elvis would sing, "I Got Lucky." We might just have a shot at this.

Now Shelby was smiling, too. "Chief Turner said the crime scene tape would come down tomorrow. What time is his flight?"

Chapter 5

After a satisfying dinner of Grottos pizza, John, Lady Anthea and I took our wineglasses into the family room. The night air was chilly, so we'd eaten in the dining room instead of the screened porch.

"Any luck finding that car?" I asked.

He shook his head. "But I'm getting closer. It was an electric car. A Kia Soul or a Chevrolet Bolt or something like that. It was bright blue with a Virginia license plate."

"Abby, look what a mess you've made," Lady Anthea said to my Standard Schnauzer. Stuffed animals, training aids, and chew toys were scattered around her bone-shaped wicker basket. My dog was rooting for something in the very bottom of the toy box. Suddenly she raised her head and looked straight at me with a stuffed blue bear covered in gold stars in her mouth. She looked pleased with herself. She gave her pretend prey a quick shake and walked off with it. Lady Anthea came around gathering up the discarded toys and tossing them back into the basket. "So, you found what you were looking for? None of these would do?" she asked Abby, with feigned sternness.

The lightness of the moment helped dispel the tension from our dinner conversation, but it was short-lived.

Thanks to technology, we had a fire in the fireplace as soon as I flipped the switch. I sat on the couch and pulled the cashmere throw that I kept draped over the back onto my lap. John joined me and watched as I tucked the blanket under my legs, crafting a cocoon. He had a scowl on his face. After studying the fire for a minute, he said, "Lady Anthea, can you tell me more about Georg Nielsen? He was here to be the guest conductor, right? The regular guy recently retired?"

I looked up with a start. "Perhaps Daniel Laurent was the *intended* victim?"

"Only in those books you read," she said. Lady Anthea patted the strand of pearls around her neck before speaking again. "Georg Nielsen is, uh, *was* the darling of the classical music world. I still can't believe he's dead. The world debut of his symphony was to be in Lewes and rumor in the music community says it's because it has an ocean theme. This symphony was to have sealed his coronation as *the* emerging talent of the decade!" She shook her head at the loss. "At first I was disappointed that Maestro Daniel Laurent had changed his mind about coming to Lewes, but to hear a never-before-performed piece by Georg Nielsen was like winning the lottery." She giggled. "Though Laurent wouldn't be keen to hear that. He was the music director and conductor of the orchestra." She took a sip of wine. "Now Georg Nielsen is dead."

"The Potomac Symphony Orchestra is still coming. We have a boarding reservation for someone's dog," I said.

"Cordy Galligan, the concertmaster," Lady Anthea said, dreamily.

"What is that?" I asked.

"The concertmaster is the instrument-playing leader of an orchestra. She's the leader of the first violin section. In this country, the position is sometimes referred to as first chair."

"Why are they still coming?" I asked. "Don't they know he's dead?"

"I reached Nielsen's agent and told him. It's up to him to tell whoever needs to know. He was going to try to reach the family in Denmark. I hope he beats the press to it," John said.

"How did this happen?" Lady Anthea asked.

"Until I learn something to the contrary, I'm going on the assumption that Mr. Nielsen drowned," he said, back to our conversation from dinner. "His blood alcohol was high. I think he passed out and fell in the water."

I shook my head. "I still say there was something wrong about the crime scene."

Lady Anthea, now seated in the overstuffed chair across from us, leaned forward. "Like what?"

"I don't know," I admitted. John huffed in exasperation. "I can't put my finger on it, but—" I looked at Abby. She had been chewing on the bear, but now she picked it up and tossed it.

"And after all that work to get exactly the toy you wanted," Lady Anthea said. Abby walked over to the bear and lay down to chew on it again.

"That's it. She was looking for a particular toy," I said. "The second victim wasn't just some sicko going through a dead person's pockets to find something to steal; he was looking for something specific. Don't you see?" I looked from John to Lady Anthea. "He knew the body was there! It didn't just wash up! Remember I told that you can't predict where a body will come to shore?"

John ran a hand over his head. He kept his hair short, almost a military cut. "The preliminary report says he drowned. And why are you looking at my hair?"

"I think someone helped him drown, like they tried to do to me. And your hair is short, but without what they call the fade. The man that was shot had the fade."

"I know what his hair looks like. We have his body."

"He was looking for something he thought Nielsen had on him and it had to be the thumb drive," I said.

"At the risk of stating the obvious, that means there's something important on it," Lady Anthea said.

"I'm waiting to get the report on that and to find out who the phone belonged to," he said.

His own phone pinged and he stood to read the text message. When he looked at the screen he said, "I'm going to have to get back to work," as he placed a call.

I stood, too. "Well, good night. See you tomorrow." The look on John's face made me regret my abruptness. Lady Anthea seemed to be caught by surprise, too. She jumped up but stayed next to her chair. She was unsure of what was going on between John and me, but then so was I. I walked past him to the living room. He followed me to the front door, now talking on his phone. We stood there and I waited for him to finish his conversation, looking at the floor, then the walls. At anything but him, though we were standing inches from one another.

"I'll be damned." It sounded like at least some of what he had heard came as news. He would file it where it belonged. I, however, left clues where I found them, since that made it easier to see what didn't fit.

He hung up and said, "We have the identity of the second victim. Name's Nicholas Knightley, goes by Nick. He was in the system because until three months ago he was in prison."

"He had a record? For what? Maybe for murder? That's what Elvis did in *Jailhouse Rock*, you know. Could he have killed the conductor?"

John shook his head. "I don't know yet. I have to go back to the station to call his parole officer." We were still standing by the front door. "There's more." He looked back to the family room. "He worked for the Potomac Symphony Orchestra."

"Whaaat?" Lady Anthea cried out in shock. I had wondered if she could hear us and now I had my answer.

We chuckled and I opened the door for him. "The classical music industry is rougher than I would have guessed," I said. "Who knew?"

He leaned closer and took my arms in his big hands. "Why am I back in the friend zone?" he whispered.

Chapter 6

At fifteen minutes after five on Monday morning, most of the town was asleep but I was parking my Jeep at Lewes Beach. I woke up knowing with a certainty usually reserved for Elvis and Grottos Pizza that I needed to go back there. Admittedly, I was counting on my attacker not being an early riser. I would make peace with the ocean since so much of my nonwork life was spent surfing and SUP, stand-up paddle boarding. I walked to the waterline, stretched and began a slow jog. I could make out the yellow crime tape up ahead, waiting in the moonlight for me to get there. To break its hold over me, I looked away and focused on the silver clouds reflected off the water of the Delaware Bay. The sand dunes stood guard on my left. They provided protection from coastal storms by absorbing wave energy and were sand storage areas ready to replenish eroded beaches after storm events. Without them, storm waves could blast inland and flood properties like those I'd thought about sending John to yesterday. Now I imagined myself shielded by them.

"Oh!" a woman screamed.

"Oh!" another woman—me—screamed back. She had been sitting on the beach and I had run over her. "I'm so sorry! I didn't see you." From her lotus position, my logical sleuth brain deduced she'd been meditating.

Because her legs were crossed with the soles of her feet facing up, it took a bit of untangling before she could stand. I saw she was a good half foot shorter than my five-foot-seven inches, and compact. Her hair was pulled back in a ponytail and she had thick bangs.

"Are you okay?" I asked. "That was all on me. I wasn't looking where I was going."

She laughed and brushed sand off the back of her yoga pants. "I'm fine. Meditating on the beach in the dark sounds like a better idea than it is." Then she laughed again, this time loud and free. "I can't believe this. I give my husband such a hard time about his technology addiction, now I had inattentional blindness because I was meditating!" She laughed some more.

"What is that? Does it mean you're as good as blind since you're not paying attention?" I asked.

She was nodding before I finished the sentence. "Exactly." She pointed at the crime scene tape over her shoulder. "What's that all about?"

"My boyfriend and I found a body there yesterday." I had never used that word to describe John before, but I liked it. Even at our ages. I let it amble around my brain. *Boyfriend.* It felt right. I just hoped he knew it. "He's the chief of police. We didn't even have our phones with us at the time and so—"

"I've done a lot of research on attention restoration theory and propinquity," she said.

Had she just changed the subject? I had no idea if that was an appropriate response to what I said or not. "You've really lost me now," I said. "Sounds interesting. Let's walk."

"I can run," she said.

"Even better." I turned around so we could head back the way I had come.

We took off jogging at a slow pace and she said, "The propinquity effect says you're more likely to form a friendship or become romantically involved with someone you're around the most. It explains workplace romances and affairs with the nanny. And having social media at our fingertips twenty-four seven on our phones gives us a sense of familiarity and even intimacy. It's not real, but it's a reason people are addicted to their smartphones. We get a positive stroke every time someone likes our post about what we had for lunch."

I thought about my friends, Lady Anthea, Barb and Red Moulinier, Jerry and Charlie, and Rick Ziegler and Dayle Thomas, not to mention all the Buckingham employees. "That can't compare with real relationships, which take work and skills, which you don't have to do and you don't have to develop with social media," I said. "What was the other one?"

"Attention Restoration Theory says your ability to focus can become fatigued in a modern urban setting, but can be restored in nature or even by entertainment, like a TV show."

I didn't want to be rude, but I couldn't help but think that was just common sense. We were at the borderline between "interesting information" and "this is why I jog alone." I checked my sports watch and saw we had been running about fifteen minutes. "I'm one of the co-owners of the Buckingham Pet Palace, and I've got to go open up."

"I'd take your number if I had my phone with me, but I don't," she said. "I don't pick it up until it's light outside. I even leave it downstairs at night because the blue light interferes with my sleep rhythms."

I had to get away before she started teaching me again. "Well, bye." I waved and turned to go to the parking lot. She did the same and walked with me through the sand, still talking. Still. Talking.

"And I sleep very well, unlike my husband." She stopped and pointed back to where I had unceremoniously run over her. "Uh, do you mind if I walk back this way?"

Did I mind? "Not at all."

* * * *

I was back home by six o'clock and Lady Anthea and I stood in the kitchen eating breakfast. I had my usual oatmeal and orange juice and she crunched on toast and sipped hot tea.

"Did you sleep well?" she asked.

Usually I was a world-champion sleeper, but not last night. I had dreamed of big, mean hands, but I didn't want to go into that. Instead I said, "I woke up thinking about how odd it is for, as you call him, the darling of the classical music world to know an ex-con."

She nodded. "It's even more surprising considering Georg Nielsen was from Denmark and lived in London most of the year."

We stood and ate for a few minutes. Finally, she asked, "What time should Mason and I leave for the Baltimore Washington International airport to pick up Albert?"

"BWI is about two hours away. You should have time to spare if you leave Buckingham's at eleven thirty. By the way, we need to tell Mason not to mention the murders." I added another scoop of raisins to my oatmeal. "Do you really think we can keep this from your brother?"

"I do! All we need to do is prevent anyone from talking about them in front of him," she said. "And it helps that he's not staying here with us."

My next-door neighbors were weekenders who rarely used their house. It was twice the size of my cottage and they had lent it to me for the duke to stay in for the week. I never let them pay for boarding or grooming their dogs and hadn't expected anything in return, but we were even steven now. The Lewes and Rehoboth Beach hotels that would be up to his high standards cost hundreds of dollars a night. I would forever be in my neighbor's debt for keeping me out of debt. The very thought of spending the week with Lady Anthea's brother stressed me so much, if I was a dog I would have chewed the sofa. Having him next door rather than in my house had gone a long way toward reducing my anxiety level.

Then a thought struck me. "I have a better idea than leaving it to chance that he won't hear about the murders. Maybe you and Shelby can take him on day trips. You can go to Cape May on the ferry one day. Then you can go to Smith Island another day and to Chincoteague." I could list many more interesting spots. I almost asked if he was a history buff, then I remembered who we were talking about and sucked in a laugh.

Lady Anthea clapped her hands. "Brilliant! That's what we'll do! But can you spare Shelby?"

"I can have Mason and Joey come out front if I need them during check-in or checkout. You know, we might just pull this off! Maybe he'll never learn our little secrets," I said. I felt my mood lift thinking of him being away and occupied every day. "I'll be ready in five."

* * * *

We had a steady stream of pet parents bringing their dogs in for grooming, day camp, or boarding, and various combinations of the three. Lady Anthea had held agility and dog-trick classes on her last visit and several wanted to know when those would be repeated. She promised Buckingham's would offer them again in a few months.

A little before eight o'clock we had a lull and I was replenishing the Twinings tea and Walkers Shortbread we kept on a table by the side wall.

Lady Anthea said, "Sue, we never discussed the second round of agility and dog-trick classes, but I would like to give them again."

"Of course! I always assumed you would repeat them. They were completely filled. Did you have a month in mind?" I asked.

She shook her head. "We have a lake on the east side of the house and it needs to be dredged. I've delayed as long as I dare. And the portico that overlooks it needs repairs also."

Shelby reached over and touched her arm. "I know this is none of my business, but have you given any more thought to using Frithsden for weddings or as a venue for meetings?"

"I think about it all the time," she said. "Albert won't hear of it." She stopped and sighed. "I can't blame all my stress on him, though. More than one dukedom has been turned down because of the extravagant costs that come with the lifestyle of a duke. He keeps going for the family."

"But neither of you are married. I mean, your husband died so you're not now," I said.

"Perhaps I should have said for the future, rather than for the family."

"So someone really turned down a dukedom?" Shelby said.

"Indeed," she said. "Winston Churchill for one. Robert Gascoyne-Cecil and Prince Louis of Battenberg were offered dukedoms and declined them because they could not afford the expenses of playing that role. The rental income that Frithsden brings in meets our expenses, but nothing more."

We took advantage of our last few minutes of downtime with an empty lobby to tell Shelby about our plan to keep the duke busy and on the road. We were discussing a schedule for the day trips when John came in.

"What are you three cooking up?"

I smiled and said, "I was about to tell Lady Anthea how beautiful Frithsden sounds."

"Maybe you'd like to see it some time?" she asked.

"Sure. Who wouldn't?" I turned to John. "And we were talking about what we could do so that Lady Anthea's brother's visit would be perfect. Any ideas?"

He shook his head and walked up to the counter.

"John, did you find out who that phone we found belonged to?" Shelby asked.

"The phone that was in the dog's mouth belonged to—"

I interrupted him. "That dog has a name. She is Bernice," I said. I didn't expect him to know that a dog has forty-two teeth, while a human only has thirty-two, but surely he could call someone who had saved my life by her name.

"Whatever. It belonged to the second victim, Nick Knightley. His parole officer verified the phone number. There's more, and after I tell you, you can say 'I told you so.' They found bruising and defensive wounds on the conductor. I admit it, that was no simple drowning."

"So Georg Nielsen was murdered by Nick Knightley?" Lady Anthea asked.

John shrugged. "Don't know yet, but it seems more likely that it was Sue's attacker, who, of course, also killed Nick Knightley."

"Oh!" Lady Anthea exclaimed. "I forgot to tell you but last night I googled Mr. Knightley, and his position at PSO was assistant librarian for the symphony."

"He was the *what*?" I asked.

"The music library is a very important behind-the-scenes aspect of a major symphony orchestra. A lot has to happen before the actual concert,"

Lady Anthea said. "Ordinarily the librarian supplies the conductor with the score and the musicians with their sheet music, but not in this case, since it's a never-before-published composition. I suppose the Potomac Symphony Orchestra would be large enough to have a librarian as well as an assistant librarian."

He nodded and said, "Well, Nick Knightley is looking less and less guilty of Nielsen's murder. First, he wasn't in prison for a violent crime. Not his style, according to his parole officer. He was a hacker, and he was doing time for internet fraud. Second, the time of Nielsen's death has been narrowed down to between ten o'clock and two in the morning. It's hard to be exact because of the salt water. He was with his parole officer in Bethesda, Maryland until after nine o'clock. If the death occurred in the earlier part of that time frame, he's not our guy. He couldn't have gotten here in time. I'm thinking the man who shot Knightley also killed Nielsen."

"Had he been turned over?" I asked.

"No," John said, reaching for my hand. "The bruising was on his chest, face and neck."

We had found him on his back. I imagined him looking up at his killer and swallowed hard.

"Now do you see why I'm worried?" John said.

I nodded. "Had the body been moved at all after he was killed? Like moved up the beach?"

"No," John said. "From how the blood pooled on the back side of his body, he appears to have been killed where we found him and in the same position."

"Then he was killed during high tide, which was around ten thirty on Saturday night," I said.

He smiled at me and waited for me to say more.

"You can't drown where there's no water," I said. "Were they able to get DNA off the fabric I got out of Robber's mouth?"

His phone rang and he said, "No, we haven't," as he answered it. I doubted he remembered the collie's name either, but he knew which piece of evidence I was talking about. He spit out a laugh. "*Bess Harper* has a *complaint* to make? I have a *complaint* for her. Don't let her leave. She doesn't need to know why. Get the interview room ready for her to be questioned about the two murders." He hung up and turned to leave, mad as hell about something. Whatever it was, I wasn't going to worry about it. I would concentrate on our plan for me to see very little of the duke and the duke to hear nothing of the murders.

"Lady Anthea? Are you okay?" I had just noticed that she was frozen in place.

John stopped and turned around.

She thawed enough to shake her head. One inch left then one inch right. "Did you say Bess Harper?" she croaked.

John nodded. "Yeah, yesterday she complained about the crime scene tape interfering with her press conference. Today it's something else. Interesting detail about her is that she called Nick Knightley at nine thirty Saturday night. The guy's in Maryland. Gets a call. Comes to Lewes, Delaware, where he's killed. And she thinks she's going to complain to *me*?" He stopped and looked at Lady Anthea and then at me. "Do you know her?"

"No," she answered. "I know *who* she is. She chairs the board of the Potomac Symphony Orchestra."

Chapter 7

"Me? Are you sure?"

"Yes, Bess Harper described you, and I quote, as a *character witness*," John, in Chief Turner mode, yelled over the phone. "Which, by the way, means less than nothing to me."

Lady Anthea and I were cleaning the inside of the mini indoor cabanas. Dogs go into these for their afternoon naps. They're also used for dogs waiting their turn to be groomed. It's a job made only slightly less unpleasant if you tell yourself it's zen, or something like that. I smiled every time I remembered Lady Anthea's first visit, when she had pitched in to help. I never would have asked her to, but she'd wanted to show she was all in. Later I learned the reason for that.

"Hey, what's that supposed to mean?" I said, a little indignant.

"I didn't mean because it's you, I mean it's not a get-out-of-jail-free card. How do you know her? And why didn't you mention it while I was at the Pet Place?"

"Pet Palace. And I *don't* know her or her character. She said she knows me?"

"She referred to you as the owner of Buckingham's," he said. "Said she met you this morning."

"Maybe she meant Lady Anthea? I'll give her the phone," I said.

I heard him trying to object but she was pulling off her rubber gloves while I put mine back on. I shrugged and returned to work.

"As I told you this morning, I know who Bess Harper is, though I've never met her," Lady Anthea said to head him off at the pass.

I was leaning into the crate and said over my shoulder, "Wait, she met me this morning?"

"He says yes," Lady Anthea said.

"I talked to someone on the beach this morning while I was running," I said.

"Did you hear that?" She had to pull the phone away from her ear because of the volume of his answer. "He wants to know what you were doing alone on the beach in the dark."

"Obviously I wasn't alone. I was with my new best friend, Bess Harper," I said to the back of the crate. I removed my gloves again and took the phone from Anthea. "Would it help if I came to the station?"

"You mean to go to lunch with her?"

"Huh?"

"First, she said she had lunch plans with you, then she changed it to she was going to ask you to lunch. She doesn't want to talk until she asks her husband whether or not she needs an attorney." He hesitated, and I imagined us both rolling our eyes at that last bit. "Obviously, she's stalling and I don't think talking to her husband is the real reason. I'm giving her what she wants. I've suspended the interview and I hope I can find out what she's waiting for." He lowered his voice and said, "I *would* like your take on this. She denies calling Nick Knightley but I know she did. Obviously she didn't kill him, since his killer was a man, but she might have the strength to have killed Georg Nielsen. She knows more than she's saying. Can you come down here?"

"Sure," I said. I wasn't wild about the idea. She claimed to want to have lunch with me, but she didn't know my name?

"Good. I told her I thought you'd be stopping by the station and that she could ask you about lunch then," he said, laughing for some reason.

"Why did you think I'd be coming there?"

His baritone laugh sounded like "Hoo, hoo." Again, I didn't get the joke. Then he said, "See you later."

Suddenly a get-into-jail card presented itself to me. "Wait, what kind of car does she drive?"

Chapter 8

As unenthusiastic as I was to leave Buckingham's to go to the police station, Lady Anthea was even less inclined. We didn't know what time Cordy Galligan was dropping off her Pekingese and she wanted to be there to welcome both, hoping they wouldn't show up while she was off meeting her brother's flight. I still wasn't clear on what a concertmaster was, but it certainly made you somebody. John had assured me Bess Harper did not own an electric-blue electric car, so she was not the driver who had picked up my attacker, and therefore had become a lot less interesting.

He strode through the lobby when I came in and hugged me. That wasn't unusual since he doesn't care what people think and neither do I, but I had been distant last night and I didn't know how he felt about that. Now here I was standing with my arms hanging by my sides. I pulled away as soon as I could. I hoped he knew I couldn't help it and that I would find my way back to him. I stalled with a question. "Were there any other calls on the phone that was in Bernice's mouth?"

"Just a couple from his parole officer. It was a burner phone and he'd only had it for a few days. It took a while to get a decent fingerprint off the phone thanks to what's its name."

"Bernice."

"Anyway, once we did it was just his own prints, so no help there."

"I wish this Bess Harper person hadn't brought me into this," I said. "I'm kind of busy."

"She thought mentioning your name would help her." He cocked an eyebrow and said, "After all, I am your *boyfriend*."

It was one thing for me to say that, but to hear it was something else. I didn't know if I was breathing or not—until I saw the look on his face. It was gentle but eager, hungry but patient. He took my hand and we walked through the public area and down a side hall.

"Why did she come in? You said she had a complaint?" I asked.

"She suspects someone was in her house when she wasn't there. Said there was sand on the floor," he answered. "I had someone go back over the reports from the neighborhood survey the uniforms did on Sunday, and she didn't mention a break-in to the officer at the time."

He opened the door to the interview room and said, "Sue Patrick, this is Bess Harper."

She twisted in her chair and grasped my hand in both of hers, greeting me like I was a long-lost friend. "Suuuuuee," she cooed. She wore a tan linen blouse and matching wide-leg pants, with strappy high-heeled sandals. My seasonal work uniform of khaki slacks and an Oxford shirt with the golf course–green Buckingham Pet Palace logo on the pocket made quite the contrast.

"Why would *I* call Nick Knightley?" she asked, like we were in the middle of a conversation. Obviously a rhetorical question, but I would have liked an answer.

I gave a little laugh, like, *why indeed.* I nodded a greeting at Officer Statler. She was seated in the corner of the room, holding a computer tablet. "Lunch?" I asked Bess.

* * * *

We walked from the Lewes City Hall building on Third Avenue to Agave, a Mexican restaurant on Second, and were seated at a table near a front window. Before we left, John had told her not to leave town without notifying him, since there was the matter of her call to Nick Knightley still needing an explanation. She maintained that she had not called him. She had her indignation but my money was on his proof.

On the way to the restaurant she told me that she lived in Georgetown, a neighborhood in Washington, DC, and spent most of the summer here in Lewes, at her vacation house on Bayview Avenue. This coveted address runs parallel to Lewes Beach, separated from it only by sea grass and brush. Her house could have been one of those I'd been looking at while I was minding the first murder victim.

"So you're here this week for the concert?" I asked.

She nodded and said, "Yes, my husband and I came Saturday. We had planned to come Monday but the pleasant weather forecast changed our minds for us. I'll stay the week."

"Did you know Nick Knightley?" I asked.

She hesitated just a beat and I got why John had the feeling she was hiding something. Maybe a lot of something. "We've met. He does work for the symphony, after all. Every encounter is unpleasant, so I go to great pains to avoid him. Whatever he's done, it has nothing to do with me."

I took note of her use of the present tense, about someone who, to be blunt, was no longer a present tense kind of guy. "How about Georg Nielsen?" I asked her.

"Pleeeease don't mention that name, either," she said. For a meditator she certainly was dramatic.

"Why not? I heard he was the second coming of Elvis."

"I hate his guts..." she said, again not sounding like someone into meditation.

"He's dead," I interrupted. It didn't seem fair to let her go on with me knowing what I knew.

Her mouth dropped open, then she tried to speak. I don't read lips, but it looked like she was saying, "Wha-wha?"

"Georg Nielsen was murdered Saturday night," I said.

"That's whose body you found on the beach? That's who you were talking about this morning?" she asked. I didn't know if I was hearing panic or drama in her voice. Then she closed her eyes and began breathing deeply and noisily. I looked around for someone, anyone, to ask what I should do, when she opened her eyes. "Wha—wha—what are we going to do about the concert?"

Not quite what I expected.

"Are you okay?" I asked.

She nodded that she was. "Sorry, I was doing my breathing exercises."

"Why did you hate him?"

"Friend-raiser," she said, in a faraway voice.

"*What?*" I said.

For the next few seconds her head pitched back and forth on her neck. I pushed my chair back so that if she passed out I could jump up in a hurry to help her. "He refused to say *friend-raiser*. You see, I prefer that to *fundraiser*." I thought about how John couldn't bring himself to say Pet Palace. He said Pet Place instead, every single time. Grinning would have been completely inappropriate, so I bit my lip.

Ms. Harper pulled a tissue from her slouchy green leather satchel. "And it wasn't just me. We met with him once after the contract was signed—you see, we hadn't begun rehearsals—but he has antagonized everyone. As chair of the symphony board of directors, I need everyone to pitch in. We work as a team. Money from ticket sales only goes so far, and we have to raise the rest. Everyone knows the realities of financing the performing arts."

"Well, there might be someone who doesn't," I said. No need to say who that might be.

"Ticket sales cover less than half of our expenses. Wait, did you say murdered?" Bess asked.

I nodded. A waitress came to take our order. "Hi, Sue! How are you?"

"I'm good. And you?" I said when I saw who it was. "How's Clairol?" I turned back to Bess Harper and said, "Her Afghan Hound has the most beautiful blond hair." Then back to my pet parent client. "How's the teeth brushing going?"

"Better every day," she said. "I did what you suggested. I rubbed her lips with my finger every day for a week and when she got used to that I started using a pet toothbrush. She mostly eats the chicken-flavored toothpaste off it, but I figure if I do it every day some is bound to get on her teeth."

"We're thinking about giving free dog teeth-brushing classes at the Lewes farmers market in the summer—"

Bess interrupted. "I'm not a dog person."

"Then let's talk about the food here." I was becoming painfully aware of the line of would-be diners at the door. "The guacamole here is really good...." I let my sentence drift off when I saw Bess was looking at her lap, and her menu was still untouched.

"I guess we need a minute," I said. The waitress gave me an *are you kidding me?* look. Getting a table at Agave without a wait had been nothing short of a miracle, and to delay ordering was a sacrilege. I gave her a little smile of apology and motioned to my guest, dabbing her nose and eyes.

Suddenly, Bess's head jerked up. "Why did Chief Turner ask me if I called Nick Knightley?" I doubted John had asked *if* she had called Knightley, but I let this dodge, or mistake, or whatever it was, go. "What does that have to do with anything?" she continued. "Wait, did that weasel kill Maestro Nielsen?"

The waitress's eyes widened, and she gave me a *what the hell?* look. I shrugged again. "I'll come back," she said.

"Thank you," I whispered.

I wanted to ask Bess why she cared. If she hated Georg Nielsen, what was it to her who killed him? "Nick Knightley was also murdered," I said.

Bess glared at me, her lips crushed into a tight line. She took a deep breath and stared down at her gold Rolex. Maybe she was meditating. I prayed she wasn't about to resume her breathing calisthenics. "I've got so much to do. Can we have lunch some other time? I believe he said that yellow tape will be gone by this afternoon?" I gave one nod and stood. The line was now out the door, having grown to eight or ten hungry people. She sprang out of her chair and headed for the door, all thoughts of lunch with her new best friend long forgotten.

We had both parked at the police station and began the short walk back there. Once we'd made a little progress down the block, I said, "Why didn't you mention that you suspected a break-in of your home during the neighborhood canvas the police officers conducted on Sunday?"

"No one came to our house," she said, looking confused.

Chapter 9

John closed the door to his office and sat in the twin of the guest chair I occupied. He put his arm over the back of my chair and smiled at me. After Bess Harper and I had said our quick goodbyes, she had practically sped away in her BMW and I had come into the city hall building.

"What?" I asked.

"I like looking at you."

"You've seen me twice this morning."

He shrugged. "What can I say?"

I told him how pitifully little I had learned in my brief visit with Bess. "So, she had come in to report someone breaking into her home?" I asked. "Could that have anything to do with the murder? I remember what you said about there being no coincidences in *real* law enforcement."

"She said she found sand on the floor of her foyer," he said. "I can't use it. Problem is, they haven't been in Lewes for months, so it could have been there for a while."

I pointed a finger at him. "Respect," I said, imitating Dana.

He laughed and leaned in. Before we connected I said, "So ask when her housecleaning service was last there."

"Respect," he said, imitating me imitating Dana.

When his face got too close, I pulled away and said, "I need to get back to Buckingham's. Lady Anthea and Mason went to pick up her brother at BWI and Shelby might need help."

We stood and he ran his hand over his head, not looking at me. "Yeah, I better get back to work, too."

"So, no DNA at all on that fabric?" I asked on my way through the lobby.

"Nothing," he said. His cell phone rang and he swiped to take the call. "The thumb drive has *what* on it?" He listened with a puzzled look on his face. "Send me what you have." He ended the call, then took my elbow and piloted me back to his office. "This might be more in Lady Anthea's line than yours, but let's look at what they found on that USB drive from Georg Nielsen's pants pocket."

I sat in his desk chair and he stood behind me, leaning over and clicking on what looked like a picture of a cardboard box on his computer screen. "This is like Dropbox for law enforcement," he said. There was a document labeled with a case number and he double-clicked on it.

"What is it?" I said. "It looks like sheet music."

"Yeah, they said it's a music score. The guy was a conductor and a composer, so I don't get what the big deal is," he said.

"The Ocean, Our Original Opus," I read out loud. "I like it."

"You would," John said, massaging my shoulders.

I twisted around in the chair. "Lady Anthea said she had heard rumors that the music they were going to debut at the concert this week had an ocean theme. I agree with you. This is what you'd expect him to have. Makes sense to me."

"Sure, it makes sense *now*. After the thumb drive dried out, they still had to find the application this was written in. They told me this is a common one used by people who write music—at least, these days."

"Duh, since it was written by a contemporary composer," I said.

"I wasn't saying Elvis used it," he said with a laugh.

"Elvis has cowriting credits on a few songs because his manager, Tom Parker, had that put in the contracts, but he didn't write any songs." Then I added for good measure, "And by the way, Colonel Parker wasn't a colonel."

John stood up straight from leaning over me and arched his back in a stretch. He pointed at the screen. "And this isn't any kind of a clue."

"Then why was Nick Knightley looking for it?"

Chapter 10

"Do you think a symphony orchestra is actually a pack?" I mused, and immediately wondered who would be its leader.

Shelby and I stood behind the reception desk. A luxury bus had driven into our parking lot and sat with the nose facing our entryway. The effect was more than a little unsettling and neither of us could take our eyes off the hood and grille of the black bus.

"I don't like this," Shelby said.

"I know," I agreed. "I thought I was just being jumpy after what happened yesterday, but it looks like it could drive right in here." I made out shapes of heads bobbing, turning, looking out windows, or slumped sleeping.

The side door had been opened by some unseen operator, then closed again. The engine had been turned off and then back on. When the door opened a second time, two people, one a man carrying a dog, and the other a woman, emerged and walked around the front of the bus and through the two sets of doors.

The man, dressed in an ill-fitting black suit and black soft-sole shoes, entered first, leading a now-leashed Pekingese. He had come in and immediately handed the dog off to the young woman, then walked back out to the waiting bus, which still sat idling aggressively—at least, it seemed that way to my imagination. She had done a double take before accepting the leash from his beefy, outstretched hand. The dog was in the normal size range for the historic breed. The coat color was cream.

"Hi," she said, walking with languid movements to the desk. "I'm Cordy Galligan."

Ah, I thought, the concertmaster that Lady Anthea thought of so highly. Her thinness was exaggerated by the skinny black jeans and black knee-high boots she wore. Her black turtleneck sweater was sleeveless, revealing muscular arms. I wondered if that was from working out or from playing the violin. She had long, black curly hair and because she glanced down at the dog every few seconds, I could see her ultrathick eyelashes.

"Abby, I'll be with you in a minute," I said. "That's my dog. She's looking at me." I pointed left to my office.

"How do you know? She didn't make a sound and you didn't look over there."

"I always know where she is and what she's doing. We've been connected like that since I got her."

I looked over her shoulder to the bus. Before the man could climb back on the bus, he had to move aside for another woman to descend the steps. She took no notice of him in her hurry to get through Buckingham's double doors. She approached the desk talking and swatting her hands in confusing gestures. "Cordy! Have you...? No, Cordy, I can't talk." The concertmaster seemed unfazed by the contradicting messages from the new arrival.

Shelby and I pulled back in tandem. Who walks up to someone and *says* she can't talk? She turned away from Cordy to face Shelby and me behind the desk, then quickly back to her again. "Have you heard from Maestro...?" She stopped and glanced at us again. She gave Cordy a conspiratorial look and with the thumb and index finger of her left hand squeezed her own lips together. Subtle. She lowered her voice, and in a stage whisper, finished her question, "*The* Maestro this morning?" This woman was middle-aged and dressed more corporately, in a red fitted sheath dress with a navy jacket. Her long, professionally straightened hair was dyed with the trendy ombré technique, with the brown locks fading to a lighter color at the ends than the crown.

My phone pinged the arrival of a text and I looked down. It was from Shelby, who stood about two inches away from me. *Who can it be? Lewes has many maestros.* I kicked the side of her foot.

Cordy Galligan shook her head. "No," she said. Her voice was so soft as to be barely audible, and the volume wasn't helped by the fact that she was addressing the dog on the floor.

"You know him, right?"

Cordy shook her head. "No."

"I've left I don't know how many messages and he hasn't deigned to return my calls!" the older woman said.

And he ain't going to, I texted back.

Shelby cleared her throat to keep from laughing. She was back to thumb-typing.

Perhaps Nick Knightley can get a message to him, I read. This time it was me who had to swallow an inappropriate laugh.

As entertaining as this was, Buckingham's was a place of business. "Ms. Galligan," I said, "this is Shelby Ryan." I checked the computer screen to get the Pekingese's name. "She can conduct Marin Alsop's temperament evaluation now, if you'd like to wait."

"What is that?" she asked in her little-girl voice.

"It's the same as a behavior test. Before a dog's first visit we want to know a little about her personality and her reaction to other dogs. It helps to ensure her safety and that of her new playmates, and to manage her stress level. We'll start with her alone, then take her to a play area to observe her with other dogs. We look for separation anxiety, toy aggression, and other behaviors like that." We had never had to turn a dog away, but I wouldn't hesitate to before I exposed other dogs or my employees to an aggressive dog.

Shelby went around to the other side of the desk and Cordy extended her arm, but couldn't bring herself to release Marin Alsop's leash. "What's the story of her name?" Shelby asked with a smile. The way she slowed down the transfer had me thinking she had noticed the hesitation in the leash's surrender also.

"Marin Alsop is the conductor of the Baltimore Symphony Orchestra," Cordy said. She knelt to her dog and said, "Bye, baby. Be a good girl." Since all was well, Shelby walked off with Marin Alsop. The dog never looked back. That's how Pekingese roll. I was thinking about what a kick Lady Anthea would get out of the name.

The superenthusiastic woman had wandered to the side of the lobby, and now she came back to the desk. She had been clicking away on her phone, texting and trying to place phone calls. Since I have doglike hearing I knew she'd left more than one heated message. She opened her mouth to say something to Cordy but her phone rang and she answered it instead. "Bess? Oh, good. I frantically need to talk to you."

I had been typing in an update for Marin Alsop's record but glanced up when I heard the familiar name, Bess. She looked at me and said, "No, wait, I can't talk just now."

Note to self: work on improving sneaky eavesdropping skills.

It took me a beat to decipher the apologetic look Cordy was giving me. Whoa. She thought I was going to leave for them to talk, or strategize, or whatever? I laughed before I could stop myself. That was so not happening. I would have to have a much better reason to leave the lobby unstaffed than to satisfy these people I didn't even know.

Cordy rested her arm on the reception desk. "This is Margo Bardot. She's the executive director of the orchestra."

"Nice to meet you," I said, but Margo, who couldn't talk, was talking to Bess and didn't respond. I wondered if I should tell them why Georg Nielsen wasn't answering his phone but decided against it, not that I could have gotten a word in.

Margo glanced at me and saw I was still standing there. She looked annoyed but continued the call anyway. "Bess," she said, "It's Maggie. I wanted to run this by you. We're dropping Cordy's dog off at the…" She looked around until she found something with our business name on it. She zeroed in on the logo on my shirt. "The Buckingham Pet Palace."

Bess must have tried to interrupt because Maggie said, "Wait, let me tell you something first. Yes, I want to hear whatever you have for me, but first let me tell you what I'm about to do. I'm going to call his agent. His," she repeated in a reverential tone, "and tell him…."

From across the desk I heard Bess Harper yell through the phone, "Maaagggie!"

"Wait! No! You're right. I'll call our attorney first! Then I'll call Maestro Nielsen's…. Oh, damn, I said his name. Anyway, I'll call our attorney and then I'll call his agent and tell him that since the terms of the contract have not been adhered to, we've decided he's in default. Do you agree? After all, our negotiations stipulated the performance of his new work."

"Noooo!" said the disembodied, but nonetheless clear, voice.

I could not begin to calculate how many hours of meditation Bess Harper was going to need to undo this little exchange.

"Oh, do you want to consult with the board first?" Maggie asked. "Of course, I should have thought of that."

I couldn't hear Bess's answer to that but the look on Maggie's face, and the fact that she was speechless, told me she was learning that Maestro Georg Nielsen had been murdered. Ignoring my inconvenient presence, she put the call on speaker and held it out to Cordy. "Say that again."

Bess Harper repeated the news about what had happened to Nielsen on Lewes Beach. I wasn't breathing; I was waiting for the other shoe to drop. The Nick Knightley shoe. When Bess added this in, Cordy took a step back like she had been shoved. Margo Bardot's eyes widened. Bess wasn't finished. "You should talk to a woman named Sue Patrick. She knows all about it."

"Who is Sue Patrick?" Maggie asked Cordy.

The concertmaster and the executive director may have looked in my direction for an answer, but I wasn't to know since I was tucked away in my office.

Chapter 11

Abby pressed her head against the side of my knee as I sat at my desk. I reached down and twirled her ears. "You're so pretty," I said. Mason had done his usual excellent job grooming her with a typical cut for a Standard Schnauzer. Her beard was long, as was the hair on her legs. She pressed against my leg again. Whatever she wanted, I hadn't yet obeyed. She wore a bandana made from fabric covered with polo ponies in honor of the duke's visit. "Want to take this off?" I asked her.

She looked at me with those big brown eyes. *Yes.*

I pulled the bandana over her ears, which were natural, not cropped, and stuck it in my pocket. "Just in case Mason complains."

I stayed in my office until I heard the double doors open. We have classical music playing in the background during business hours and switch to Elvis at one minute after seven. The volume was kept low enough not to interfere with my eavesdropping on what was going on in Buckingham's lobby as they made plans to make a statement to the press. Cordy said very little, which made sense. It was my understanding that the business side of the orchestra was the responsibility of Margo, or Maggie, as executive director, and Bess as president of the board, who was still on the phone. When I came out, they hadn't made much progress in deciding whether or not to cancel the concert. And the bus was still parked across our parking lot.

Lady Anthea came in, followed by a rather tall man with strawberry-blond hair. Mason brought up the rear. He walked around the group and as he passed me on the way down the hall, he mouthed, "You owe me. Big time."

I was still looking at his retreating back, wondering what had happened during the return drive from the airport, when he turned and looked back.

He waited until he caught Lady Anthea's eye. Then he grinned and gave a little half bow. Mason and Joey had a firmly entrenched tradition of bowing whenever they saw Lady Anthea. She told them that her title didn't warrant the gesture, but they kept on and now it was like their secret handshake, and made her giggle every time.

As Lady Anthea and her brother approached the desk, Cordy and Maggie retreated to the side of the lobby where our small boutique was located. I smiled at the duke, but he wasn't looking my way. He squinted as he examined the lobby, then looked over at the two women from the Potomac Symphony Orchestra, not attempting to hide his curiosity. It was fine with me that he hadn't yet been bowled over by my charms, since now I had a little time for my quandary. I seemed to remember that reaching out to initiate a handshake with royalty, like the queen or a prince, was boorish, but what was the rule for dukes? They were, after all, the highest-ranking hereditary peers. His sister had been entangled in *two* murder investigations—one that he knew of and one he didn't—thanks to me. Not to mention the current body count. I figured my reputation was starting as a negative number. I wanted to get this right.

Shelby returned with the Pekingese. "Lady Anthea, let me present Marin Alsop," she said. She glanced at the duke, who was still scanning the room.

Lady Anthea looked down and said, "Welcome to Buckingham's. Lovely to meet the first woman conductor of a major symphony orchestra!" She laughed and petted the small dog's head, then she rose and looked around for her brother, who had wandered off to stand near Cordy and Maggie.

Shelby took advantage of Lady Anthea's diverted attention to mouth, "Is that him?" as she nodded in the direction of the duke.

I nodded and whispered, "The Duke of Norwall." Then I grabbed my phone to google my etiquette question but soon had to stop to eavesdrop.

"We have to make a decision!" Margo was saying.

"We don't have a conductor, so we should cancel and go back to DC *now*," Cordy answered, finally adding her two cents and speaking in the direction of the phone in Margo's hand.

"We may have to," Bess said. "We can't bring Daniel Laurent back. He's the guest conductor for the Bath Symphony Orchestra for the season. I was surprised he accepted the invitation since that's an amateur orchestra, but he took it because this is their seventieth anniversary year."

Cordy nodded but didn't speak.

"Uh, aren't you Cordy Galligan?" the duke asked her, practically breathless.

Neither woman appeared to have heard him and he took a step back. He clasped his hands in front of his body and seemed okay with waiting to be acknowledged. There was something about the way he stood that made me think of a schoolboy.

Finally, Cordy lifted her head. "We might appear, well, insensitive if we go ahead with the concert."

"He was one of the most famous conductors in the world," Margo said. She spoke slowly, like she was hatching a plan. "After this week's performance, *celebrated composer* was certain to have been added to his name, too. Perhaps we could perform his piece to honor him." By the end of the sentence her voice had taken on a dreamy quality. "If only we had a conductor."

"Ladies," the duke said, "allow me to introduce myself. I'm Albert Fitzwalter, Duke of Norwall." He had moved forward and gave a slight bow. Thanks to the way he'd identified himself, he had their attention. "I'm at your service. I shall be happy to be your conductor."

Lady Anthea lurched forward onto the reception desk. "Sue!" she gasped.

Cordy and Maggie looked around the duke to me, one craned around his right arm and the other around his left. "You're Sue?" they asked in unison.

Chapter 12

Lady Anthea was whispering something to Shelby and me, across the reception counter. "We have to stop this!"

Cordy and Maggie glanced at the duke, then looked at one another, exasperated and conspiratorial, acquiescing to the reality that they would have to deal with this fan before they could find out what I knew.

"Are you a conductor?" Cordy asked. The skeptical expression on her face said that if he was, it wasn't with a major symphony orchestra or she would know him—and she didn't know him.

Maggie examined him with narrowed eyes, then began thumbing her phone at lightning speed, occasionally looking back at the duke. Oh yeah, she was googling him. I didn't hear anything from Bess and I imagined her dual-tasking on her phone, also checking Albert's online presence.

"Sue?" Lady Anthea hissed. "Did you hear me?"

Nodding, I whispered, "There's no way he's not going to find out about the two murders if he spends time with them."

She mumbled something that sounded like, "I wouldn't be so sure of that."

"Huh?" I asked.

"A double murder is nothing compared to some events that have escaped his notice in the past," she said, keeping her voice low, "but can we chance it?"

Shelby answered her, "Yeah, we need to stick to our plan to keep him out of town with day trips."

"He has absolutely no idea what's involved in conducting an orchestra," Lady Anthea said.

"He knew who Cordy was, so he must know classical music," Shelby said.

"I couldn't have picked her out in a lineup," I said.

"Of course we know who Cordy Galligan is!" Lady Anthea said.

Maggie's phone was talking so I turned my attention to that conversation. Bess said, "Thank you, and…"

At the same time Cordy said, "Thank you, but…"

Two very different futures had been laid out. Bess won. "It would be our pleasure to have you as our honorary guest conductor," she said.

"Why can't he still be gone all week? The murders should be solved by the night of the performance," I whispered.

Lady Anthea shook her head and squeezed her eyes shut. "Most of the work is done prior to the concert. He'll be with them all week."

Cordy spoke again and we turned our attention to that group. "That's asking a lot of you," she said. "I doubt you have time for our *daily* two-and-a-half-hour rehearsals." She had emphasized *daily* like she was writing it in blood. "You're probably very busy."

"Not really," he said.

"Every day," Cordy added, in case the word *daily* had a different definition in the United Kingdom.

"That's perfectly fine," the duke countered.

My phone pinged, informing me I had a new text message. "This is from John," I told Shelby and Lady Anthea. "He says Bess is going to make a public statement on Lewes Beach in about half an hour."

Lady Anthea clutched her pearl necklace. "Are they going to announce that?" She tilted her head toward her brother.

"I'm sure they'll at least talk about Georg Nielsen's death!" I said. "Keep him busy and away from Lewes Beach!"

Shelby wagged her head side to side. "He's still going to find out."

"We can at least buy a bit of time. When it occurs to him that this could be real work, maybe he'll change his mind." Lady Anthea walked over to join her brother.

After introducing herself to Cordy and Maggie, she took him by his arm. "Let's get you settled in." She turned him around and he let himself be led in the direction of the door. She called to me over her shoulder, "We dropped his luggage off earlier, so we'll walk."

His glance back offered me a couple of seconds to look at him more closely. He did look dog-tired from traveling. Hopefully he would nap like an old dog in the sunshine or Abby on a car trip when she was a puppy. I waved a hand to say goodbye but he was scanning the lobby again and looking down the hallway, and didn't see me.

His departure took care of one of my problems, although only temporarily. It was just a matter of time before Maggie and Cordy, who were still in the lobby, whispering over in the corner, remembered Bess's advice to talk to me about the murders. I hadn't thought about the attack in hours, and now I realized how I'd compartmentalized the murders in one part of my brain, and the man's hand holding my head underwater in another. Nielsen's and Knightley's murders I could talk about, but the attack on me was marked, Danger, Do Not Enter. "Shelby, I don't want to talk to them."

"Maybe go to that," she said, pointing to a side door with a raised eyebrow.

* * * *

I grabbed a sweatshirt, my car keys and handbag, and blew Abby a kiss before slipping out one of our side doors into a playground filled with a pack of puppies supervised by Taylor Dalton. The young woman usually worked as a nighttime hostess taking care of boarding dogs, but had started picking up extra hours as a nanny, which is an employee in charge of the puppy playroom.

Turns out the stealth wasn't needed, because by the time I chatted a few minutes with Taylor and got to my Jeep, the orchestra's black bus was on Village Main Boulevard. Its turn signal did its job and indicated it would be making a left onto Savannah Road, the direction of downtown Lewes. Cordy and Maggie must have exited the lobby right after I had. Two cars separated me from the bus as we drove along the two-lane road. During the tourist season I inched along, but today we could drive at the speed limit, which started at thirty-five and decreased in seriously enforced increments as we neared the downtown historic district. They might have been headed to their hotel or to the beach, or a lot of other destinations. I had never thought about what musicians did when they weren't on stage. Lady Anthea could have filled me in. My phone rang and the screen on the dash said it was her. "Hi!" I said. "What do musicians do in the daytime?"

"What?"

"I'm following the orchestra's bus and I was trying to guess where they're going."

"They could be going to rehearsal," she suggested. "Do you know where that will be?"

"No idea. We're still on Savannah Road and we've passed all the hotels and the streets that lead to them, so if they are staying in Lewes, they're not going to their hotel. One possibility is the press conference Bess Harper is holding on the beach. Or they could be going to her house."

"All of them?" she asked.

"It's a big house," I said. "I just got my answer. They drove into the parking lot at Lewes Beach."

The driver stopped the bus diagonally across several parking spaces in the row nearest the sand. I parked as far away from it as possible, at the street entrance, and continued my narration. "They're all getting out."

"My brother is asleep. I walked back to Buckingham's. I'll get Mason or Joey to bring me to the beach. I'd love to hear what they say." The Prius we use for door-to-door service for pet parents who chose to have their dogs picked up and dropped off was available, but Lady Anthea's driving would have to get a lot better before I could make that offer. "Wait, I believe Shelby needs to talk to you."

I watched as the musicians filed off the bus. Margo, her phone to her ear, was first, followed by Cordy. The group congregated, circling Cordy, and seemed to be waiting for instructions from her. Finally, the driver disembarked, hauling some odd-shaped aluminum equipment. He went to stand behind Cordy, never taking his eyes off her.

In the background I heard Shelby say, "Lady Anthea, I have a question for *you*. I have Bess Harper on the other line. She wants to talk to your brother. What should I tell her?"

"No!" I yelled.

"Tell her he's resting and is not to be disturbed," Lady Anthea told Shelby. Then I heard her say, "Mason, would you take me to the beach?"

"Why? Going surfing with Sue?"

She laughed, and I imagined her tapping her pearl choker, a gesture now familiar to us.

"Ahhh!" I jumped and tossed my cell phone into the back seat. John had rapped on my car door. "You scared me to death!" I said as I got out. When I retrieved the phone I saw Lady Anthea had already hung up.

John and I swung around at the sound of a car. The BMW driving from Bayview Avenue had a large, loud engine. Parking in a space by the entrance to the lot no longer seemed like a good idea. He pushed me behind his back and against the Jeep. The car made a sharp right turn onto Savannah Road, skidding, almost fishtailing, in the sand that coated the beach parking lot.

"Was that Bess Harper?" I asked from behind his shoulder. "She drives a white Beemer." He was pressing against me one second and gone the next. With fluid and powerful movements, he ran to his car, taking the Lord's name in vain a couple of times on his way. He folded his tall frame behind the wheel and was gone. From the crook of his neck I knew he was calling other officers. The sound of his siren traveled up the street and stopped within seconds when he pulled the car over. The BMW driver was toast.

I looked over at the orchestra and realized if Bess had called Buckingham's looking for the duke, I should make myself scarce in case Maggie Bardot got the idea I could serve him up. I climbed back in the Jeep.

Meanwhile, Maggie and the bus driver were scouting spots to set up for the press conference. He lugged the metal contraption to one spot and then to another, impassively doing her bidding. The height of his load made it cumbersome, especially walking in the sand, and he didn't seem a fit man, but his face was a blank. Ten or so paces onto the beach was considered and rejected. The two trudged back in the direction of the parking lot, but Maggie stopped in front of a white wooden bench, halting him with a hand outstretched to her side. They had a winner. The contraption turned out to be two metal sculptures of music notes. He unfolded each one once and then again. Including the stands, they stood six feet tall when he finished. He placed one on each side of the bench. Now and then a musician glanced over to check their progress. As frenetic as Maggie was, they were serene.

Lady Anthea and Mason drove in and pulled up next to me. She got out and Mason stayed in, nodding at me. Once she was in the Jeep, he left to go back to Buckingham's.

I updated her on what I'd been surveilling. "Pretty boring stuff," I said to sum it up. "There's Jane and Michael Burke from the *Southern Delaware Daily.*" We watched the couple join the group of musicians. Michael paused to snap a photograph or two. The spontaneous scene—some musicians leaned against the bus, many wore jeans, a few fingered imaginary instruments—would make an artistic tableau, but our local newspaper didn't do artistic. What was Michael up to?

More reporters joined the group. "It appears the press conference will be well attended," Lady Anthea said. "And thankfully, one person will not be here. He's sound asleep."

Maggie was on her phone again, but she was standing next to Cordy now. The bus driver stood guard at the bench but looked over at Cordy time and time again.

"The only excitement we've had was a BMW that came speeding through, possibly driven by Bess Harper," I said.

She raised an eyebrow. "I wonder where she was going."

"Wherever it was, she was going in a hurry until John pulled her over," I said and we laughed at her misfortune.

I looked at my phone to get the time. "I wish they would start." Next I looked at my side mirror to check the Savannah Road traffic. "Speak of the devil." The BMW was back, still speeding and again skidding on the sandy asphalt, the driver obviously not chastened. The car blew by us so close the Jeep rocked.

I held my breath and Lady Anthea let out a squeal at how near it came to the musicians before coming to a stop.

Bess got out, confirming my suspicion that she was the driver.

"Oh, no!" Lady Anthea and I said at the same time.

Albert had gotten out from the passenger side. Maggie walked up and he allowed her to lead him to stand to the left of one of the giant music notes.

"They weren't unorganized. They were just waiting. How did they find him?" I was already reaching for the door handle to get out of the Jeep.

Lady Anthea and I walked across the parking lot. "He knows," she said.

"Yeah, we have to assume he knows about the murders," I agreed.

She nudged my elbow and motioned for me to move to the side of the group, so we could stand in front of the speakers. Four musicians had climbed onto the bench and the others stood in curved rows in front of them, like ripples in a pond.

"You weren't able to talk him out of conducting the orchestra?" I asked.

"I tried." She shook her head. "He has no idea what's involved."

"There's got to be a lot more to it than waving your hands like you're writing the letter *L*, but other than that, I really don't know what a conductor does," I said.

"First, the motion is keyed to the tempo of the music being played. The shape isn't an *L*. The movement used for four beats per measure might look like the number four, and represents a quick tempo. A conductor does so much more. An *inspired* conductor *inspires* his or her musicians. He or she brings out unexpected brilliance." Her words were spoken with emotion.

Sure, I could have used more details, but I wasn't a complete Neanderthal. "That's the tempo for "Don't Be Cruel.""

We were walking and she stopped watching her brother just long enough for an eye roll at my comment. "He'll pat his tie three times," she said.

"Is that a code? Like he's trying to get a message to you?" I asked.

"Huh? No," she said.

"Something similar was used in *The Southern Shotgun*, the mystery I started last night," I explained.

"Please, Sue, I can't listen to the titles of those books you read just now," she said, pinching the bridge of her nose.

"It's destined to be a classic."

"Or anything having to do with Elvis Presley, who is not the king of anything."

We stood in the sand in front of the makeshift stage. Bess now held a small wireless microphone. She and Maggie stood in front of the group and she cleared her throat, the universal signal for everyone around her to shut up.

"Good afternoon," Bess began, which was the cue for the lone television camera to begin filming. The bus driver held up his phone to video her. She introduced herself as the chair of the Potomac Symphony Orchestra board. "You may have heard that the music world lost a shining light over the weekend. Conductor and composer Georg Nielsen was to have debuted his masterpiece *Symphony by the Sea* right here in Lewes!"

Cordy was standing in the first row of musicians, at the left end of the line. She jerked her head at what Bess said and the quick movement caught my attention.

I leaned over to ask Lady Anthea if she had noticed Cordy's reaction, but changed my mind when I saw what her brother was doing. He patted the button of his navy sports coat, then his tie. He repeated the gestures two more times. "He did it," I said. "What does it mean?"

"He's uncomfortable," she said, drawing it out.

"Really? I'm pretty sure he's scared," I said. That might have been a little harsh, but I was still smarting from what she had said about Elvis.

Bess went on, "We, as members of the Potomac Symphony Orchestra family, believe we've found a way to honor his memory in an extraordinary manner. To tell you about that, I'd like to introduce Margo Bardot, our executive director and stage manager."

Maggie took the microphone and beamed a smile at the small audience. "I'm delighted—" She froze. "I mean, I'm sad. Uh, what I mean to say is that I'm sad *and* I'm delighted. I would say, uh, I would say—"

"Oh, no." I knew I was about to go into a laughing fit and there wasn't a damn thing I could do about it.

"I would say she's wrapped, and not wrapped, herself in a good and proper knot," Lady Anthea said behind her hand.

Maggie had hit on a way to express her opposing feelings, and gave a nervous laugh. "You might say I'm relieved. Yes, I'm *relieved* to announce that the performance will be conducted by Albert Fitzwalter, Duke of Norwall."

I turned to the Delaware Bay behind me and saw John walking my way. Could I nonchalantly walk to the water? Would I have time to get away before I cracked up? The answer was no, and I fake-coughed to hide my laugh.

John was at my side, "Ma'am, am I going to have to arrest and not arrest you?"

Lady Anthea turned her back to the stage, too. She was fighting a losing battle to keep from laughing. She tried to keep her lips closed, so when the laughter came out it sounded like, *puh, puh.* She dabbed her eyes.

I took a deep breath and chanced a look back at the stage. Maggie held out her shaking arm and Albert came forward, smiling. His face displayed contradicting emotions, like a man who wanted to run for his life, but not leave.

He nodded and smiled, first to the right, then center and then left, at the smattering of people, applauding politely. He patted his tie again and began, "Good afternoon."

Lady Anthea had turned to face the stage. "How do you think he's doing?" she whispered.

"Can't you see him? Want me to scoot over?"

"I was curious to know what *you* thought. Do you think he's handsome?" she asked.

I knew to be diplomatic, but that's about all I knew. John leaned forward a bit to look at Lady Anthea, then at me. When our eyes met, we telegraphed our mutual confusion. "Sure, in a duke kind of way."

"What?" she said, clearly as confused as I was as to what I meant by that.

"When he talks, only his lips move," I said, keeping my voice low.

"Isn't that how everyone speaks?" she asked.

"It's like the rest of his face has the day off," I said.

She was laughing again. *Puh, puh.*

I was laughing. John was laughing. We managed to keep the volume down but our three sets of shoulders bobbed like we were on the high seas.

"I'm here today with my sister. Anthea, please join me. She's the owner of the Buckingham Pet Palace."

Chapter 13

Her brother's invitation for Anthea to come to the stage sobered us up fast. She didn't go forward. Instead she'd smiled graciously and waved. "Sorry about that," she said when the crowd turned their attention back to the speakers. "He knows I'm barely a co-owner and you do ninety-nine percent of the work."

I shrugged off both his comment and her apology. We'd never had a moment's confusion about our arrangement. Our contract allows us to use her name and likeness and that of their estate, Frithsden, in exchange for a portion of the profits. Last year she conducted dog agility and trick classes to help pay for a new roof for their Grade I listed house. Between our research and our conversations with Lady Anthea, Shelby, Dana, Mason, Joey and I had learned a bit about Frithsden's history. First, it was pronounced Friz-den. Next, it was in the Greek Revival style—it was designed to look like a Greek temple, the Theseum in Athens, to be specific.

Albert was speaking again. Earlier at Buckingham's I'd seen him from the side, and now at the beach he was directly in front of me. He told us how happy he was to be in "historic Lewes" and how "friendly and welcoming everyone" had been. I didn't know if his unoriginal comments were because he wasn't a going-out-on-a-limb kind of guy, or from the fact that he'd been in town less than twelve hours, and didn't know any more than that about us.

I looked around at the small audience and noticed two men who were neither photographing nor recording the event. One wore designer eyeglasses and was in the process of switching them out for the sunglasses version. "Who are they?" I said it aloud, but to myself.

"Who?" Lady Anthea asked.

"Those two men look very familiar to me, but I can't place them," I said.

Lady Anthea tilted her head to look discreetly. "They were in the driving skills class yesterday."

"Oh, yeah!" The friend with the stubble wore a different flannel shirt today. The guy in the specs wore a different cashmere sweater. Today's was navy. "You were still in the puppy room when the guy in plaid blew up at Charles Andrews," I said.

"Can you blame him after he told them to, and I quote, 'grow a pair'?" she asked.

John chuckled and his deep voice must have carried, because both men looked at us, then moved away.

"What I want to know is how stubble can look the same every day?" I asked. "It gives new meaning to the phrase, 'it's five o'clock somewhere.'"

Albert thanked the group again and turned to hand the microphone back to Bess Harper, who in turn offered it to Cordy Galligan. She smiled shyly and raised a slim hand to her neck. *No, no,* she mouthed.

My phone pinged that I had a new text message. I took it out of the pocket of my khakis and saw it was from Dana, who was back at school. She had forwarded an image of a man and woman leaving an ornate, historic-looking building. I gasped.

"That's Cordy Galligan," Lady Anthea told John. "She could be from another time."

"How do you mean?" John asked.

"She's so demure and innocent." This could have been followed by a dreamy "ahhhh." She was entranced.

"Oh, yeah?" I held out my phone for her to see. She took it from my hand and examined the photo more closely. Her eyes widened, then closed, and she gave the phone back to me. I handed it to John.

"This is her?" he asked, pointing first to my phone and then to the improvised stage. "When was this taken?" he asked through clenched teeth.

"It says Saturday," I answered, already forwarding him the photo of Cordy Galligan and Georg Nielsen walking arm in arm. "They were coming out of a restaurant in Manhattan. When she brought her dog to Buckingham's, I heard her tell Margo Bardot she didn't know him."

He paused just long enough to run his hand down my back and was gone. I watched him until Lady Anthea spoke. "Seeing the man the day he died doesn't mean she killed him."

I shook my head. "No, and remember he was killed in Lewes and she only got here today." I looked at my screen again and noticed that while the conductor was smiling broadly, Cordy's smile was tight and hadn't reached her eyes. Not even close.

Lady Anthea and I went back to looking at her brother.

"Should we be worried about him?" I asked.

"I won't pretend to not know what you mean," she said, certainly more aware of her brother's limitations than we were. And we were well aware. I doubted she knew that Shelby, Dana and I google-stalked his every move, ridiculing his silliness and shallow, pompous public remarks. His poor management of Frithsden was the reason Lady Anthea had entered the partnership with me. That much she'd shared during her first visit to Lewes. "Everything we've learned about the two murders has led back to the Potomac Symphony Orchestra," she was saying. "And he's going to be with them all week."

Bess Harper had the microphone that Cordy had turned down. "We *all* hope to see you at the concert on Friday night!" She emphasized "all" and lifted her arm, indicating the rows of musicians standing behind her.

We applauded, politely, and when the group of musicians dispersed, the reporters descended on them.

"Let's go," I said, striding through the sand toward the group. "We have to get busy."

Lady Anthea nodded, again not pretending she didn't know what I was talking about. We had murders to solve.

I whispered, "Does public speaking make your brother nervous?"

She shook her head *no*.

"Then why does he seem so uncomfortable?" I asked.

"He's worried about who will find out and what they will think," she said.

She was talking about the Royals.

Chapter 14

Lady Anthea finagled an invitation to tea from Bess Harper, using her brother as bait. John had proof she'd telephoned Nick Knightley on Saturday, although she swore blind she hadn't. Plus, she had expressed an intense dislike for both of the victims. All Lady Anthea and I had to do was gently nudge the conversation to Georg Nielsen or to the symphony or to her whereabouts on Saturday night or Sunday morning, and we'd have clues, known as evidence to the boys in blue. Easy.

We walked diagonally through the Lewes Beach parking lot to Bayview Avenue. Strips of grass surrounded a square, raised porch, which was the entrance to their at-least-million-dollar home. Bess stooped and tilted back a foot-high statue of a frolicking dolphin. She slid the hidden key out and unlocked the door.

Lady Anthea and I, along with an untalkative Albert, sat around Bess's dining room table as she worked in the kitchen. We were on the second floor of the townhouse, not the entry level, which was a layout that offered a nice view of the water from the balcony and the rooms on that floor. The walls of this room and the living room were lined with modern art, but I didn't dare walk around to look at any of it. I felt like the room was holding me hostage. Bess had told us the paint color on the walls was ultra violet when she apologized for the smell caused by the recent redecorating. Ultra *violent* would have been more like it.

The dining table was made of repurposed whitewashed pine planks, and the centerpiece was a tall, simple vase filled with seashells, interspersed with black-and-white plastic shovels for making sand castles. The fun decorative accessory was nonthreatening, so I focused on that.

Albert still hadn't spoken to me. I'd tried making conversation with him as we walked to Bess's house but he had pretended not to hear me. I was curious about why he was snubbing me, but I didn't really care.

I whispered to Lady Anthea, "I'm not ashamed to admit I'm a little afraid of the color of these walls." They were aggressively purple.

"It's really horrible, isn't it?" Oops. Bess had come in with the teacups and overheard me. Here was someone who now had the right to be standoffish. It wasn't like Albert had caught me saying anything like that.

"I'm sorry," I said, reaching for a china cup. "I know next to nothing about decorating."

"But, Sue, your house—" Lady Anthea started.

"Really, it's okay," Bess interrupted. "My husband has these two rooms repainted every spring with the Pantone Color of the Year. So at least I'll only have to live with it for one season. Or that's how it usually is."

"Ordinarily, you're only here in the summer?" I asked, working my way to the topic I was interested in.

"That's all the time I've had to spare since I was elected board chair for the symphony," she answered.

"But for this visit you came, uh, when?" I asked.

"I'm here this week for the concert."

"So it was you who suggested Lewes as the venue?" I asked. The symphony orchestra's home was Washington, DC. Why had they come all the way to Delaware?

"Is your husband a decorator?" Albert asked, taking the cup Bess offered him and unwittingly veering the conversation to something inconsequential. Actually, he'd T-boned my questioning.

"Oh, no, he's an IT guy." She paused and bit her lower lip. "At least that's how he started. Now he's a venture capitalist. A few months ago a magazine article called him a tech mogul and he loved it." She gave a little laugh, but the way the volume of her voice had trailed down to nothingness left me wondering if *she* loved it. "Anyway, he says colors are equations and he has to have the very latest."

The front door opened and we all turned to see who would come up the stairs.

"Roman," Bess called out, "come meet our guests. We were just talking about you."

The man in the cashmere sweater and eyeglasses had already turned to escape to the home's third floor. I felt Lady Anthea's eyes on me. He was Bess Harper's husband. That explained his appearance at the press conference. Seeing no way out, Roman stopped and joined us in the dining room. He plastered a smile on his face and repeated each of our names as we introduced ourselves.

"I apologize for Charles Andrews," I said when it was my turn to introduce myself. "He can be pretty tough. We've all gotten used to it." Though he and his friend in the flannel shirt had been younger than everyone else in the driving skills class, I noticed he was about a decade older than his midforties wife.

"Who?" he asked.

"Let me see, how can I describe him?" I asked.

It turned out I wouldn't have to because the front door opened again. "Anyone at home?" The voice was young and the question had been spoken word by word. *Any. One. At. Home.*

Bess was on her feet. "Up here, darling." She turned to us. "That's our daughter, Sophie."

Roman smiled and reached his arm back for her. The teenager came far enough up the stairs for us to see her face before she stopped to sneeze. After that she sneezed on almost every step. When she reached the dining room her father gave her a stiff-arm hug. The young teenager wore an undercut hairstyle. The hair at the nape of her neck was supershort, almost shaved, and black. The top had been pulled into a ponytail and dyed blond. She had a cupid's bow mouth and porcelain skin—which was perfect, even after the sneezing.

"Is there a dog in here?" she asked as she looked around. Again, with the staccato cadence, leading us to mentally hear question marks in the middle. *Is? There. A. Dog? In here?*

"Maybe she's allergic to us," I said, motioning to Lady Anthea.

Bess seemed to be intently studying her offspring, but didn't say anything.

"We'll go upstairs," Roman said and led her up to the third floor. To Sophie he said, "Looks like they've been feeding you well at that school."

Bess's face colored at her husband's mean comment to their daughter. Albert looked from one person to another, seemingly unaware of the strain Roman had left in his wake.

"Can we see the view from your balcony?" I asked in an attempt to rescue Bess, getting up from my chair.

"Sure," Bess answered, giving me a grateful smile for the distraction before she walked over to open the sliding glass door.

"That would be lovely," Lady Anthea said.

The balcony was small but the view across the Bay and down the length of the beach was spectacular. I took in a long, slow breath to recalibrate my senses after the assault by the wall color. When I was ready to reenter the world, I pointed to a nearby spot to our north on the beach. "I ran into Bess right there. Literally. I was jogging and I didn't see her."

"It's true!" Bess laughed along with Lady Anthea, but it seemed forced. Perhaps she was still embarrassed by what her husband had said, and I wouldn't have blamed her. "I was meditating and had my eyes closed."

"So your daughter goes to public school?" Albert asked, not twigging that we were pretending we hadn't heard Roman Harper's cruel comment.

"No, she goes to a private school in Massachusetts."

Lady Anthea said, "Our public schools would be referred to as private schools here, though these days most people refer to them as independent schools to avoid the confusion." She went on to describe the different types of schools in the United Kingdom.

We stood and looked out at the view for a few minutes until Lady Anthea asked, "Shall I help you clear the dishes?"

Her brother followed her inside and I would have gone in also, but Bess stopped me with a hand on my arm. "I'm worried," she said.

Good. Finally, I was going to hear something about the murder.

"Something about Sophie has changed every month since she started going to that school. Now she's talking like English isn't her first language. Roman wants her to have everything he couldn't have as a child."

I tried to hide my disappointment at the subject matter, but thought it was good that she was confiding in me. Even better that she wasn't asking for my advice. "I don't know anything about children, but maybe she's just experimenting with who she wants to be."

"Maybe," Bess said.

She didn't make a move to go back inside, giving me an opening to ask her about the phone call that she either did or didn't make, instead of talking about kids or paint colors.

Before I could get a word out she said, "There's something I wanted to ask your help with. It's a legal matter, you see."

"Yes?" I tried to keep the hopefulness out of my voice.

"Can you take care of this speeding ticket your boyfriend gave me?"

Chapter 15

The walk back to the Jeep and the drive to Buckingham's could generously be described as awkward. I tried asking Albert, now in the passenger seat so he could be comfortable, direct questions, to which he gave one-word answers without looking at me. Lady Anthea tried to make conversation from the back seat, without much better luck. We drove at the speed limit along Savannah Road in a line of cars, and what should have been a short drive seemed crazy-slow because of the tension in the car.

"Isn't this traffic a little heavy for the off-season?" Lady Anthea asked, gamely.

"Yes, it is!" I said, my enthusiasm for the topic over-the-top. "These are cars that just disembarked from the ferry."

"The ferry!" she said, like we were discussing a promising cure for cancer. She told her brother about the ferry connecting Lewes, Delaware to Cape May, New Jersey. Somewhere in between the factoids of the trip taking eighty minutes and transporting both cars and foot passengers, I stopped listening. She had taken to our little beach town right away. What was with this guy?

I felt Albert's eyes on me. He stared at me from the passenger seat like he had something to ask or tell me, but then his expression morphed into that of a sneaky kid with something up his sleeve. I focused on the road ahead and felt sad. Lady Anthea did not deserve this, but you can't choose your family. Her sense of duty meant she would carry him for as long as they lived.

We stopped at a red light on the bridge over the canal and I checked my phone for texts or messages. Shelby and Mason had tried to reach me. It seemed they wanted to talk to me, *ALONE*, both had written, in shouting, capital letters.

I had planned to ask Albert if he wanted to go to Buckingham's with Lady Anthea and me, or back to my neighbor's house. After that text I made the decision for him. I turned right into Villages of Five Points, but passed the Pet Palace and kept driving.

"Uh, uh," he sputtered.

I accelerated and within minutes we were pulling into my neighbor's driveway.

I smiled and said, "We'll pick you up for dinner after we close at seven."

He looked back at Lady Anthea, but she twirled her fingers in a wave. "Toodle-oo," she said.

He climbed out of the car, and before closing the door begrudgingly grumbled to Lady Anthea, "Toodle-oo."

She exhaled a sigh of relief as he walked to the front door and let himself in. "Did you know that's slang for à tout à l'*heure*, which means "see you soon" in French?"

"Nope, I didn't," I said with a laugh. Now that her brother was out of the car I should tell her about the texts from Shelby and Mason, but I didn't. Instead I asked, "How do you think Georg Nielsen got to Lewes from New York City?"

"Could he have driven?" she offered.

I nodded. "Depending on the route, it would take about four hours to get here. So, yeah."

"In that case, his car would be here. Maybe Chief Turner could check the streets around where he was found."

My phone rang and I could see on the dash screen that it was John. "Hi," I said. "Lady Anthea and I are headed back to Buckingham's."

He hesitated, then returned my greeting, but his "Hi" seemed off. Like it was a question. One he didn't want to ask. "I just wanted to give you a heads-up that I'll be bringing Cordy Galligan in to talk."

I rolled my eyes and mouthed to Lady Anthea, "Here we go again."

"I know you're thinking I'm jumping to conclusions," he said.

"That's exactly what I'm thinking. Cordy ended up in DC and Georg Nielsen ended up here."

"How do you know she went back to DC?"

This time Lady Anthea spoke up, since John was about to question one of her music heroines. "She came in today on the bus with the rest of the orchestra."

"And her dog," I added, like this proved anything. "We were wondering how Mr. Nielsen got to Lewes. Did he drive?"

"He doesn't have a driver's license. I'm assuming someone brought him and that's why I'm bringing Cordy in for a talk."

"Nielsen could have taken the ferry." We were at Buckingham's and I parked. Lady Anthea opened her door, then saw I hadn't made a move to get out, and waited. I was stalling for time, using the phone call as my excuse. If what Shelby and Mason wanted to tell me had to be kept from her, I wanted to postpone hearing it.

"I can go over the ferry passenger list for Saturday night," John said, "but I'll still need to talk to Ms. Galligan to piece together his movements."

Lady Anthea told him about tea at Bess Harper's house.

"Did you find out anything, or were you planning on holding out on me?" he asked.

"Fair," I said. "That was the old me."

"I know," he allowed.

"I can vouch for there being nothing to withhold," Lady Anthea said. "We learned nothing."

"I'm not so sure. It seemed to me that house held a lot of secrets." I told him about learning that Bess's husband was the man involved in the near-altercation with Charles Andrews. "I'm not sure what to make of Bess."

"What do you mean?" he asked.

"Her husband makes the decisions on everything from paint colors to their child's school. She disagrees but it seems like she doesn't have a say in any of it. Lady Anthea, did you get the same impression?"

"Not really," she said. "They seemed like a normal family." I looked at her, wondering how our take on the Harper family dynamics could be so far apart. I wondered if she had noticed it, too. "Sue, what you saw was compromise," she said as soon as we said our goodbyes and hung up with John.

"I think both Bess and Roman Harper are under that general anesthesia known as money."

"Are you sure this doesn't have anything to do with how *you* feel about marriage?" she asked.

Chapter 16

Lady Anthea had a routine of walking in the afternoon in England, and most days she did the same in Lewes. Shelby, Mason, Joey and I huddled around the reception desk to talk.

Shelby began. "*Duke* called here and said he wanted copies of our profit and loss sheet. We think that's the same as a profit and loss statement."

"He told me the same on the ride back from BWI," Mason said apologetically.

They waited for me to say something. "You mean Albert?"

Three heads nodded. "Does he know what that is?" I asked.

They shrugged.

"We have a profit and loss statement?" I asked.

"We have bank statements," Shelby said.

"And tax records," I added.

"Maybe the accountant has it?" Joey asked.

"Beats me," I said. "Lady Anthea hasn't said anything about this." I remembered how I'd found her on Sunday, looking preoccupied and a little anxious. Was this why? Wouldn't she have given me a warning? "Did he say why he wanted it?"

"I asked him and he said he wanted to conduct an accounting, which I think is the same as an audit," Mason answered. "I told him you were probably the best business person I've ever known."

"I appreciate that. What did he say?"

"Nothing," Mason answered.

"I think that's why he asked me next," Shelby said. "Lady Anthea hasn't said anything about that?"

I shook my head. "We're a small business, growing every year, and in the black every year. It'll be fine."

"I'm afraid for my beloved filing system," Shelby said.

"Let's kill two dukes with one stone," I said. "Tell him he can have a meeting with our accountant. That'll keep him busy and out of our hair until the case is solved."

"Whew," Joey said, relieved. "He would make a mess and I doubt he would know what he was looking at." He, Shelby and Dana had set up and refined a system for computer records and hard copies so that any employee could step in and work at reception when needed for check-in or checkout. Everyone did his or her part to keep order.

"We have a lot of dogs coming through here every day and errors are almost nonexistent, thanks to our system. We've got to keep him— Shhh, here comes Lady Anthea," Shelby said.

Mason turned to go back to the grooming suite and motioned for Joey to go with him.

"Wait!" I said. "Nothing's changed in our relationship with Lady Anthea. She's our friend. And *she's* my business partner, *not* him. We can't let Albert come in between us and we certainly won't let him alter the way we run Buckingham's. If he brings it up again, tell him to see me."

My cell phone rang as she came in.

John launched into the reason for his call. "Nielsen wasn't listed as buying a ticket for the ferry on Saturday night. I've been looking at the onboard security camera footage in case he was a passenger in someone else's car."

I interrupted him. "You sound so stressed." The silence on the line lasted long enough for me to suspect he'd hung up. I looked at my phone and the timer clicked off seconds. "Are you there?"

"Uh, yeah. I can't seem to catch a break on this case. Every case has an entry point. There's always something the perpetrator did wrong that becomes a piece of evidence that leads to another, then another, but not this case. Usually there's some loose thread to pull on."

"You have two loose threads. You know that Bess Harper called Nick Knightley on Saturday night. And you know that Cordy Galligan saw Georg Nielsen on the day he was murdered," I reminded him. Or was I trying to reassure myself? I couldn't tell him how badly I needed him to solve the murders, because I'd gone from seeing the hand with the gun next to my face when I closed my eyes to feeling the pressure of his hand holding my head underwater and his knee on my back.

"Neither one is enough to make an arrest," he said. "Anyway, I found him on the video footage, and at one point it appears a woman is talking to him but it's hard to tell, and even if he is, I have no way to ID her. See what I mean?"

"Yeah."

"No Elvis wisdom for me this time?"

"No-o-o," I said.

"What's on your mind?" he asked.

"Everything has led back to the Potomac Symphony Orchestra. Everything. I was thinking that Lady Anthea might have some insight if she saw the footage of Georg Nielsen on the ferry."

"There's not much to go on, I warn you, but do you two want to come in and look at the video? I mean, unless you're going to be with Lady Anthea's brother?"

"What time should we be there?" I asked.

Chapter 17

I told Lady Anthea about John's request and she readily agreed to come with me to the station. I was hoping she would bring up the subject of her brother's request to go over our books and maybe even open up about what was behind it, but we both were quiet for the drive to downtown Lewes. That wasn't like us. Could she have questions about how her share of the profits was calculated? If yes, why hadn't she said so?

"I hope you'll try to get to know my brother this week," she said, finally.

The comment surprised me. Surely, she'd noticed how arctic he'd been. I mumbled a meaningless, "Mmm," before shifting the subject a little. "How did Bess know where to find Albert to bring him to the press conference?"

"I have no idea. Did I mention where I was taking him when I extracted him from Buckingham's?" she asked. She turned in her seat to face me.

"No, you said you had dropped off the luggage and that you'd walk. That would have told her the general location, but it's a big subdivision."

I parked and as we walked to the door she said, "Let's ask him at dinner tonight."

John walked across the lobby and ushered us to a nondescript meeting room. His touch was so light I could have imagined his fingertips on my back, if it hadn't been for the way his eyes lingered on mine. We sat at a round wooden table and Lady Anthea and I swiveled our chairs to face the laptop computer, situated to give all three of us a good angle for viewing. He dropped his cell phone on the table and pulled the keyboard and mouse closer. The movement woke the screen and he clicked to play the video.

"Did you just keep looking until you found a guy wearing a tuxedo?" I asked.

"Yup," he answered. His phone lit up showing he had a text.

Having no choice, I read it. It would be rude of me not to. I'd worry about the logic of that later. It was from "Mom." I knew she was a famous character actress, now of a certain age. She had linked an article from the press conference and written, *You have an honest to God duke in that 1 horse town?* She had substituted an emoji for the word "horse." *When are you going to get out of there?*

"Are you two done?" The baritone voice startled me.

"Sorry," I said, moving my eyes off his phone and on to the computer screen. Wait, he had said "you two." I looked over at Lady Anthea. She looked sheepish, but that wasn't all. The wheels were turning. What was she up to?

"Sue? You've yet to meet Mrs. Turner?" She pursed her lips and looked at John and then at me before demurely turning her gaze down to the table. "Oh, we-l-l-l-l-l."

I stared at this friend-stranger-extraterrestrial alien.

John coughed. "I'll fast-forward to the times I spotted him." After a minute or so he stopped on a man in a white shirt with a bow tie hanging limply around his neck. Georg Nielsen's head was turned to the left, which gave us a clear view of his strikingly handsome face.

"What is he looking at?" Lady Anthea asked, leaning over the table to get a closer look.

"I think I know where he is on the ferry, and he's probably just being careful and looking where he's going. He's in one of the passageways going from one side of the vessel to the other," I answered.

The next time we saw him his chin was raised. "Now he's looking for someone," John said. Nielsen was striding through the food court.

"He's not alone. He's already with someone," I said.

"How do you figure?" John asked, looking at me.

The smirk on the young man's mug wasn't my clue. "Where's the jacket to his tux? He left it with someone," I said. In my peripheral vision I saw John's slow smile. "He's on the second deck. I can see it's dark outside, so he was on the six o'clock ferry?"

"Yeah," John said. "Here's the time stamp."

He placed the cursor on the corner of the image and we read, *6:55 p.m.*

Lady Anthea checked her watch. "Don't we need to leave soon for dinner?"

"That's really all there is here," John said, pushing his chair back and getting up.

"He never talks to anyone?" I asked.

"There's one more sighting." He sat back down and fast-forwarded to another image.

We watched as the conductor entered the bar and walked straight up to a chair and sat down. His companion was seated under the camera and his or her back would have been against the wall. We couldn't see the person, but there was definitely someone sitting and waiting for him. Georg Nielsen shook his head. He picked up a glass. *No,* he mouthed.

Chapter 18

"I have a confession to make," Lady Anthea said when we were in the Jeep making our way up Savannah Road back to Buckingham's.

"You murdered Georg Nielsen?"

"Very funny. After you told me who John's mother is, I've been looking her up on the internet regularly."

So, while Shelby, Dana and I had been googling Lady Anthea's brother, she had been doing the same for John's famous mother. That was karma for you. "Did you learn anything good?"

"She's getting more parts after a long hiatus, but hasn't had a new husband in years."

"He told me that when she agreed to take grandmother roles she started working again," I said.

She hesitated, then said, "It hasn't struck you as a tad odd that you haven't met her?"

Lady Anthea's curiosity was what struck me as a tad odd. We had become friends—good friends—while sidestepping the most private parts of our lives. I didn't know if that stemmed from our personalities or her British reserve, or because we're not teenagers. The exception was when she'd asked me why I had never married and I told her I'd seen too many examples of people cruelly hurting one another. "I guess I never thought about it."

"Do you think she'll ever come here to see her son?" she asked as her phone bleeped.

"I doubt it. Obviously, she's not a fan of our town," I said. I desperately wanted to ask her what she wasn't telling me. Her out-of-character behavior had started with her comments after we read the text from John's mother. No, that wasn't right. I had first noticed a difference on Sunday.

"This is a text from Albert." She shook her head and gave a moan of frustration. "He wants to stay in this evening."

"That's fine," I said, meaning it was more than fine. "He's probably tired from his flight and wants an early night." I wasn't in the mood for his silent treatment and would have preferred to talk about the case with Lady Anthea. "Carryout?" I offered. "Lots of options. Does your brother like seafood?"

"I seem to remember that's the same as takeaway. I'll telephone him. Who needs noisy, crowded restaurants? A night of conversation would be lovely," she said, with enthusiasm and what sounded like relief, for some reason.

As she talked to Albert she elevated an evening with carryout food to the ranks of previously unheard-of elegance usually reserved for the gods. When she finished she paused for him to respond. Suddenly she screeched, "What?! We most certainly will not bring yours to your door and leave!" She fumed as he argued and I wished the call was on speakerphone. "You are perfectly safe! We will see you after we close Buckingham's for the day." She ended the call, closed her eyes, and rubbed her temples.

"So he definitely knows about *both* murders?"

She nodded and her eyes were still closed. "What you must think of him."

"I haven't been around him enough to think anything of him, and why would my opinion matter? I just had an idea. If he's worried for his safety, we can invite John to come to dinner, too."

"That's not quite what I had in mind," she said.

When we got back to Buckingham's it was almost seven o'clock, time to go upstairs to say good night to the part-timers and the boarding dogs. "Let's go up," I said to Abby. That was the command for her to leave my office and come down the hall. She's not allowed to walk freely in the lobby because I didn't want pet parents to think they could have their dogs off-leash at drop-off. She walked to the elevator and stood to press the button.

"Is that a new trick?" Lady Anthea asked with a laugh.

I nodded and patted Abby. "Good girl." The door opened, and we got on for the one-floor trip. "I want to check on Marin Alsop and see how she's doing, in case she's having any separation anxiety."

Taylor was on the phone when we got out of the elevator. "I was just calling Shelby. Look." She pointed to one of our smaller rooms. The Pekingese was lying in the corner. She didn't seem stressed, but she wasn't happy and she was lethargic. Her chin rested on the floor and she followed the conversation with bulging brown eyes.

"She hasn't been like this all day, has she?" I asked, even though I knew someone would have alerted us if there had been a problem. I walked in and knelt down by her. I waited for a sign she wanted to be petted. She inched her nose closer to me. That was my signal and I scratched the top of her head.

"The day crew said she kept to herself. Other than not playing with the other dogs she was fine. She's not a very active dog, but she—"

Abby walked in and butted my hand away. Marin Alsop raised her head and watched to see what my Standard Schnauzer, a larger dog than herself, was up to. Abby bowed, showing the Pekingese she wanted her to get up and play. Marin looked at me and then back at Abby.

I'm waiting heeeere.

Marin got up and took a step forward to sniff Abby's bearded face. My dog raised her snout a little and literally looked down her nose at the new kid, then before I could grab her she took off, with Marin Alsop in hot pursuit.

I stood up and watched the two run a lap around the boarding suite.

"Should I get Abby?" Taylor said, with a laugh.

"Let's see how this plays out," I said.

"Look what Abby is doing," Lady Anthea said. "She can run much faster but she's keeping to a pace that Marin Alsop can run." We watched as the dogs began lap two.

"Taylor, are there any notes on her profile about her being shy?" I asked.

She went to the corner desk, picked up the computer tablet and swiped away. "She is in a one-dog home, without children, so she might be tired from this much stimulation."

"She's slowing down, so maybe she is fatigued. Is she to board?" Lady Anthea asked.

Taylor nodded, still reading. "She's here for day camp and boarding. It says that Cordy is staying at the Hotel Rodney."

"They have some pet-friendly rooms," I said. "That would have saved her some money."

"But none are available, so M.A., that's what we started calling her, will be here until Cordy lets us know her checkout date."

"Can I see that?" I moved around to look at the tablet screen over her shoulder.

"Why don't we call Cordy and ask if she wants her dog to come home with us and spend the night there?" Lady Anthea asked.

"I'll text her," Taylor said.

"Sure. Abby, come." My dog looked at me and I could see the wheels turning in her large brain. She ran up to the elevator and stood. "Abby!"

Chapter 19

On Tuesday morning Lady Anthea, Shelby and I stood at the reception desk and strategized. Albert's first day as guest conductor would start in two hours, at nine o'clock. He had requested to be "knocked up" at half past eight. Knowing that meant he wanted his sister to wake him up lowered the ickiness factor about a millionfold, though it did nothing for the sloth factor.

I had been up since five. Cordy Galligan didn't respond to Taylor's text so Marin Alsop had stayed at Buckingham's with the night nannies giving her extra attention. Shelby had brought her down to the lobby to be with us and texted Cordy that her dog had slept well. Now she stood by my leg. Abby was in my office but keeping an eye on what was going on at the reception desk. I reached down to pet the Pekingese. "Marin Alsop is a mouthful. Do you mind if we call you M.A.?"

Hearing my voice, Abby got up from her bed and came out. She nudged M.A. and walked to the hallway, where she was not allowed to go without me. I followed both dogs to see what was going on. Abby walked up to the elevator, stood and pressed the button. She lowered herself and backed up and sat. Someone was going upstairs, and it wasn't going to be her.

* * * *

The symphony orchestra had reserved the neighborhood community center for their rehearsals. Lady Anthea explained that the acoustic properties of the room made it a perfect choice, with its high ceilings and generous size. I had assumed Albert would be okay with the five-minute walk from my neighbor's house to the rehearsal, but I had been wrong.

"He wants to be chauffeured?" Shelby whispered. "Are you kidding me?"

I assured her I was not. "At least the late start is convenient. The morning rush will be over."

"We're going to use the nine o'clock start to our advantage," Lady Anthea said. "When we take Albert, we'll stay and learn what we can about the musicians."

"Maybe one of them knows why Georg Nielsen came to Lewes on Saturday instead of Monday with everyone else," I added. "If the desk gets busy, text me and I'll come back. I might even walk the quarter mile." I would be looking at hands, but I didn't want to say that out loud.

Shelby pushed back a ton of curly red hair and checked her sports watch. "I'll leave at seven thirty to pick up Robber and be back in plenty of time." We have a number of dogs who use our door-to-door service, but Robber's pickup time was the earliest.

At seven o'clock we opened the doors. It was showtime. Three cars were in the parking lot and the pet parents were hooking leashes on their pets' collars to lead them in. Shelby and I handled check-in and Lady Anthea stood in the middle of the lobby greeting both humans and dogs. I smiled, thinking what a good sport she was. She was a big part of the Buckingham Pet Palace's success.

Mason and Joey were on their way in, but waited and held the door open for more pet parents.

"Tell Kate that today is on us. That dog will forever be one of my favorites," I said.

"Good!" Shelby said with a thumbs-up. "I still can't believe what she did."

"You might say she took a bite out of crime," Joey said.

We groaned as Mason bowed to Lady Anthea.

"On that note, I'm out of here," Shelby said.

On her way through the double doors she passed someone who was the opposite of a pet parent, namely John. Everyone in the lobby called out some form of greeting to him.

"Morning," he said back. He took off his sunglasses, and I saw the warm way he was received made him smile all the way to his eyes. I thought about the text from his mother. He was a part of Lewes and she didn't even know it.

Mason and Joey had turned to go to the grooming suites to begin the day, but stopped when John called out, "Mason, can you hold up?"

He came back to the desk and John asked, "Did anyone report a dog bite? Sunday afternoon? Or even Monday?" He was still holding his Ray-Bans, and was putting them in his inside jacket pocket when a plastic bag fell out. Mason stooped to pick it up. He examined the enclosed blue fabric before handing it to John.

"I'd say ninety-eight percent cotton and the brand is probably Saint Laurent. Very expensive. Italian-made, not this year. Sorry, no dog bites to report." With that Mason walked away, leaving all of us with our mouths hanging open.

"Impressive," John admitted. "Too bad the only DNA we got was the dog's."

* * * *

Lady Anthea had followed her eight thirty wake-up call to her brother with another fifteen minutes later. At five minutes before nine, we parked in my next-door neighbor's driveway and waited. He came out of the house looking like an unmade bed, though one with expensive sheets. He wore a navy blazer with brass buttons, gray slacks, and black leather loafers. He finger-combed his hair as he got in the Jeep. "Good morning," he said.

"Did you sleep okay?" I asked.

"Yes, I did. Thank you for asking."

Since I was backing out of the driveway I looked in my rearview mirror. I caught Lady Anthea following this meager exchange with a level of interest it hardly warranted.

Maggie Bardot met us at the walkway to the clubhouse. "We only have one fob to unlock the door, so I've been acting as doorman."

The duke chuckled politely and I picked up on a bit of nervousness. We went in and found ourselves immersed in chaos. Folding chairs were arranged in semicircles in one half of the large space, but no one was sitting down. Here and there instruments had been abandoned. It seemed that every single person was talking. To me it was a roomful of hands and my eyes flew from one to another, looking for a match with my assailant's.

The bus driver unfolded music stands and arranged them in the rows, one for every two chairs.

"I wonder why he's doing that?" Lady Anthea mused.

"So the sheet music won't fall on the floor?" I joked.

Albert boomed a laugh, leaning over to slap his knee.

She rolled her eyes at us and said, "Do they not have a stage manager?"

"Margo Bardot is the executive director and stage manager," I said.

Now the bus driver placed sheet music on each stand after carefully inspecting it. The thickest stack of pages was reserved for the conductor's stand.

"The conductor has the score, and each musician has their part," Lady Anthea explained. "The librarian supplies them."

We were still standing in the unoccupied half of the hall, trying to be inconspicuous. Albert stood with us, wide-eyed but silent. Lady Anthea leaned near him and said, "Should you introduce yourself?" To me it sounded more like a suggestion than a question. He shook his head no. Margo looked our way and gave him an encouraging smile. When he didn't budge, Lady Anthea gave his back a gentle push. No one else had seen it and it was just enough to make him take a few steps forward in the direction of the orchestra. After a few tentative steps he was standing in the middle of the room, still a good ten feet from the chairs. Maggie had joined Bess Harper and they stood in the doorway of the kitchen looking out. The bus driver was now waiting in the back corner of the room behind the musicians.

The waiflike Cordy Galligan appeared to glide out of the kitchen as she stepped between the two women. She had a smile on her face but didn't seem to be looking at anyone in particular. The musicians raced to put their paper coffee cups on the nearest table, or toss them in a trash can. Cordy walked to the first chair in the front row and stood there looking into the middle distance. Suddenly, magically, every musician was seated, instrument in hand, waiting. No one spoke. She nodded to an African American man seated in the center of the middle row. His instrument was the oboe. He raised it and played one perfect note.

"He's playing A440," Lady Anthea whispered.

A cacophony of instruments being tuned erupted. When it died down, Cordy sat and looked at Albert.

Chapter 20

Albert cleared his throat and walked to his music stand. He read the top page, turned it over and studied the next sheet.

"Notice how many more pages the conductor has? It's because he has the score," Lady Anthea whispered. She was repeating herself. Was she nervous, too?

"The 1812 Overture?" the duke croaked.

Cordy raised her violin to her left shoulder and the other violinists followed suit. Her bow hovered over the instrument. Lady Anthea didn't seem to be breathing as she waited for her brother to do something, anything. He raised his right hand and when he lowered it, the musicians began playing. It was obviously a familiar piece and I couldn't tell how much attention they paid to Albert, if any. Cordy glanced up at him, then quickly looked back to her sheet music. Albert was drawing an *L* in the air. Of course he was. Just like everyone does when they imitate a conductor while driving or showering. The motion was unconnected to the pace of the music they played.

Lady Anthea pulled my arm. "Let's go."

I was more than happy to go back to Buckingham's. Though we wasted no time getting to the door, we were a few seconds too late.

One minute the violin bows were moving up and down in unison, then they were at every height. The timpani player was first to revolt. He yelled to a group of musicians in the string section, "Are we or are we not playing the 1812 Overture?" Some of the musicians in the string section responded to his assault with rolled eyes and others with grumbling. Then his supporters in the percussion section began stamping their feet.

Emboldened he went on, "Then can we perhaps play it at the proper tempo? If anyone knows what that is!"

A cellist came back with, "You were there, so I'll defer to you!" His string section compatriots cheered and stamped *their* feet.

A young woman whose *one* job was to operate a metal triangle picked it up and furiously ran the wand around the three sides over and over, leaning closer to the timpani player's face with each lap. The less aggressive musicians lowered their instruments to their laps and looked about in confusion.

All the musicians were yelling. No, not everyone. Cordy sat poised and silent. She ducked her head to study the sheet music on the stand she shared with her neighbor violinist, staying above the fray. Her curly hair fell forward and she tucked it behind her ear, giving me a view of her face. The smirk she was trying to hide spoke a symphony. "She could stop this if she wanted to," I said.

I motioned to Lady Anthea to go out to the porch. She pulled the door closed behind us, but turned back to look through the glass and check on her brother.

"I have never seen anything like that and I can't unsee it," I said. We could still hear the brawl but at half the volume. I turned my back to the door and looked up at the sky.

"I'm surprised it doesn't happen more often with that many egos in one room," she said. "Since these musicians are with a major orchestra, they are the best of the best. They've played the 1812 Overture numerous times and would naturally have their own interpretation. It's up to the conductor to, uh, *convince* them to conform to his or her preference for how the piece should be played."

"Do you think your brother knows how he wants it played?" I asked.

"I doubt it."

"Do you think he would be able to influence those musicians if he did?" I asked, pointing to the group.

She shook her head. "Sadly, no."

"They were mad at each other, not at him. Why was that?"

"They wouldn't dare," she said. "Even a *guest* conductor is held is high esteem—"

Suddenly the room went quiet. She and I looked at each other with raised eyebrows.

"You think it's safe to go back in?" I asked.

She nodded and inched the door open.

Cordy was standing, facing Albert. "*The Ocean, Our Original Opus* from the beginning." She turned to the oboist and nodded. He produced that all important *A* note. By the time she was seated, it seemed all was forgotten and forgiven. "Maestro?" she whispered.

Albert looked at her and she motioned to his stand with her bow.

He looked down and exclaimed, "Oh!" A baton had been left on the stand and he picked it up. He tapped it quickly and the musicians readied themselves. Albert tapped again.

The opening notes were slightly hesitant, like someone walking very slowly. I imagined someone who had never seen the ocean drawing near the surf.

"I need to get back to Buckingham's. We're not learning anything to help with the case," I said. Before I could ask Lady Anthea if she wanted to stay there with her brother, or return with me, the music changed. Now most of the instruments were called in and for a second the music became motion, or at least that was my perception. I looked around at the concentration evidenced by the musicians' strained facial expressions. Some raised their eyebrows, some lowered theirs. Lips were either flattened into a tight line, or pursed in a pout. Cordy alone remained unruffled.

I stood transfixed in the open doorway. I experienced the ocean the way I felt about it before my attack. Then I felt someone's gaze. The bus driver stared at me from his post at the wall behind the orchestra. His look said *I understand.*

Albert shuffled some of the papers in the score and two fell to the floor at his feet. As proof that meaningless conducting was better than none at all, the orchestra once again fell apart. The few musicians still valiantly playing had their own tempo in the cacophony. Just like that, the spell was broken.

Chapter 21

"Margo Bardot is holding for you. She says it's urgent," Shelby said, from my office doorway.

"After an hour of paperwork, I could use a little excitement," I said. "I'm tempted to ask what isn't crucial for her, but come to think of it, the last time she was hysterical was when she learned she had a dead conductor and no one to lead her symphony orchestra." I reached for the blinking light.

"Sue, I'm here with Cordy and Bess. You've got to help us!"

Does Cujo have you trapped in your car? "How can I help?"

"It's about this morning's rehearsal…." She let her voice drift off.

They had me on speaker. I, however, held the receiver tight to my head since I was expecting Lady Anthea and her brother back from lunch any minute. "It was pretty bad, wasn't it?"

Shelby was behind the reception desk and in my line of sight. She waved her arms and mouthed, "They're coming." I nodded.

"It was a disaster!" Maggie said.

Bess spoke up. "We don't want to cause any offense to His Grace."

"This has put all of us in an awkward position, hasn't it?" I hadn't heard the doors open, but I kept my voice down.

"Exactly!" Cordy agreed. "It's not too late to cancel the concert."

"Now, Cordy, we've been through all that," Maggie cooed.

The door opened. "That was a delicious lunch!" Albert said.

"I'm glad you liked it." Shelby had recommended the neighborhood seafood restaurant.

"At home, I would take a nap about now," he said.

I turned to face the window behind my desk. "Could you come to Buckingham's to brainstorm? I'm sure we can think of something," I whispered.

"Of course," Bess and Maggie said at the same time. "Can we come now?"

The duke was talking again. "Perhaps instead of a nap, I could have a tour of the facilities?"

Shelby cleared her throat and coughed. I nodded to show that I got the message.

"On second thought, could I come to you?" I casually offered, though I was really pleading.

"Huh?" Maggie said.

"Would you like to come to my house?" Bess asked.

"I'll see you in a few minutes. Cordy, should I bring Marin Alsop to see you?"

The pet parent was about to answer, but Bess interrupted. "Oh, I'm afraid not." I knew sorry-not-sorry when I heard it.

I told them I'd see them in a few minutes and went out to the reception desk.

"Sue!" Lady Anthea said, like she hadn't seen me in years. "Albert was just saying he'd like a tour. There's no one better for that than you!"

"Me? I was just headed out."

"I can do it," Shelby said.

"Allow me," Mason said in a smarmy tone I knew better than to trust. He walked around the corner. "Sue, I need to look at something in your office before the guided tour."

He walked around me and nodded. I took the hint and followed him back. "What's going on?" I asked.

"I have a few minutes before my next client so I'll give him a tour. Maybe he'll say something about why he wants information on Buckingham's financials. Why did he and Lady A want to have lunch *alone*? Whose idea was it?"

"I don't know who suggested it, but I assume they wanted to discuss that rehearsal debacle. It was obvious he didn't know what he was doing and he's embarrassed," I whispered.

Mason chuckled and shook his head. "Shelby told me what happened." He looked over his shoulder in the direction of the lobby, then asked, "Does he seem even slightly humbled? No. He's trying to get her on his side."

I thought about how he'd sounded and had to agree with Mason's assessment but not his conclusion. "I think you are confusing obliviousness with cunning," I said.

"What did he say when you told him that he couldn't see our records?"

"I haven't told him. He hasn't asked *me* for them," I whispered.

"Ugh, I was going to be good cop, but if you haven't been bad cop, how can I?" He brushed his black hair away from his face with a heavily tattooed arm.

"So be in-between cop," I suggested.

"That's not a thing."

"No?"

"No. I'll still be good cop," he said. "I'm not sure how to be bad cop to someone you call Your Grace and Sir." As he turned to go back to the lobby, he bumped into Lady Anthea.

"What's this all about?" she asked.

Mason apologized for almost knocking her over and gave her his secret-handshake-bow, then went to Albert. "Sir, let's tour."

The rest of us watched them walk away. "Lady Anthea, Bess and Margo want to talk about this morning. Would you like to go with me?"

"That's only fair, I'd say." She motioned down the hall. "Since he's here because of me."

I looked down at Abby, so innocent on her dog bed. "No, Mason doesn't need your help with the elevator button."

Mason was saying, "So how does this duke business work?"

"Well, there are royal dukedoms and nonroyal dukedoms. Mine is the latter."

"Ya don't say."

"The first nonroyal dukedom was created in 1448..."

Chapter 22

Margo stared at me in disbelief. Then she looked at Bess and waited for her to weigh in, but it appeared she wasn't ready to commit.

"Cordy, what do *you* think?" I asked the phone in the middle of the table. The four of us sat around the tan wicker table on the Harpers' balcony. I had been surprised to find that Cordy wasn't with the others when we got to Bess's house. Margo had told us she was at the hotel resting.

Lady Anthea said, "This just might work." During the drive along Savannah Road I had laid out my plan. The shock had finally worn off and she had recovered the ability to speak. "I thought it was crazy, too, when I first heard it." I didn't know if that tepid endorsement warranted my gratitude or not. I doubted it.

"I know you usually rehearse for two and a half hours four times before a concert, and this is asking a lot," I said.

Finally Cordy spoke. "You want us to rehearse in the morning with her brother, and then again at night?"

"With you leading the second session," I added.

"This just might work," Maggie said, echoing Lady Anthea. "But, of course, Cordy, only if you agree. Of course, it's not unheard of for a concertmaster to conduct an orchestra."

We waited for the concertmaster to tell us whether or not she'd go along with the plan. If she had been there with us, we could have gone inside and the purple walls would have worn her down.

Maggie continued, "Having Georg Nielsen conducting his new piece would have given the PSO new life. Next year our orchestra will celebrate our seventieth! If we can pull off *this* concert we can fundraise—" She stopped and looked at Bess. "I mean, *friend-raise* by showing our patrons that we can still surprise them!"

Bess gave her a smile of appreciation and asked, "Would the night rehearsals be at the same venue?"

"That would be too close to us and Albert might hear you," I told them. "I was thinking of the library if they will allow us to be there after-hours. They close at eight o'clock. Lady Anthea and I can go there now and reserve one of their meeting rooms."

"Do they have one large enough?" Margo asked.

"This morning you had, what, fifty musicians?" I asked.

"Yes. We have one hundred permanent members, and we brought fifty-two," she answered.

"I guess now that we've had the press conference, it's too late to cancel," Cordy said.

Maggie leaned over to speak closer to Bess's phone. "Why would we want to, now that we have, uh, a solution to our problem?"

Lady Anthea's face colored and I spoke up. "Albert's intentions were good. He was trying to help."

Finally Cordy relented. "Looks like I need to let everyone know we'll be rehearsing tonight."

Margo and Bess sighed in relief. We hung up just as Roman pulled into the driveway and Bess waved down at him. "Hi, darling," she called over the railing before we went inside.

He gave her a peck on her cheek and said, "I'm looking for Ty. I got us a tee time." He picked up the phone she had just placed on the dining room table and gave its gold case a disgusted look. He then dialed, not thumb speed-typing, but stabbing the numbers with his index finger. "He's not answering." He hung up and sent the phone skidding down the table.

The walls were starting to get to me and I headed for the stairs. "We'll let you know if we have any trouble reserving the space."

* * * *

Lady Anthea and I drove through downtown Lewes to the library, taking the fork in the road to the left off Savannah Road at the Zwaanendael Museum.

She said, "Do you really think the library will let us hold the rehearsals after they close?"

"I've been texting the library director. She's a friend of mine. Look at all these cars! I wonder what's going on?"

We found a parking spot near the back of the lot and made our way to the entrance.

"What is speed dating?" Lady Anthea asked. She'd stopped and pointed to a large sign. *The Check-out*, it read. *Literary Speed Dating.*

"I've heard of libraries hosting these. It's for singles to meet. You talk to someone for a few minutes, then you move on to the next person. They write down the names of anyone they want to see again and turn it in. If it's reciprocal the host shares the info—" I stopped when I saw the three long rows of tables, each consisting of four six-foot tables placed end to end. So many men were talking and using hand gestures! They waved, reached, and pointed.

"Would you care to register?" a young woman who had come up behind us asked. She was conservatively dressed in black slacks and a white sleeveless top but wore a delicate gold nose ring. She wore no eye makeup but you could almost see your reflection in the thick layer of red lip gloss.

"Oh my, no," Lady Anthea said.

"Yes," I said.

"I'll register, too," a baritone voice behind me said. I turned to see Chief John Turner. We each took the form the librarian handed us and moved to the counter to complete them. No one spoke.

"I'm here to look at all these hands. I know I'll recognize his hands when I see them," I said.

He shook his head. "No, you won't. You have no idea how fallible human memory is."

"I'm not saying my memory is as good as, say, Abby's. But it's not bad. What are *you* working on?" I asked.

"I got the ballistics report on the bullets. I'm working on that. From your description of the gun, he was using a suppressor. That helped."

"My description?" I had to laugh at that. About all I knew was that it was a gun. John and Officer Statler hadn't pressed me, which might have made me *remember* what I never saw. My drawing of the firearm was only slightly more detailed than a stick figure.

"Suppressor? What is that?" I asked.

"Same as a silencer."

"But I heard the shots," I said. "They weren't silent."

"It's not like on TV. A suppressor reduces the sound by a few decibels. That's all."

"What about the electric-blue electric car?" I asked.

"Yeah, I'm looking for the car, too. You were just at Bess Harper's house. Did you learn anything?"

"How did you know that's where we were?" Lady Anthea asked. She was rarely unhappy with John—actually, she was quite a fan of his—and encouraged our relationship when I dragged my feet.

Instead of answering her question, he said, "And I'm keeping an eye on Ms. Galligan. I either do that or I bring her in to ask about her relationship with Georg Nielsen," he answered. He saw the looks on our faces and said, "Not for his murder. I don't think she could have held him down to drown him, even though he was intoxicated. Just for information."

"You sure about that? Have you seen her arms?" I asked.

He leaned in close to me and whispered, "Can I see you tonight?"

"I'm busy," I said. I would have said more but suddenly there was a disturbance at the end of the middle table, and it included a bark and a growl. In a library?

So-Long was on Charles Andrews's lap and the dog was sending a message to someone in the front of the room. I turned back to John, but he'd gone. The young librarian was back. "If you're going to participate, you'll need to sit down. There are a couple of openings at the first table." She pointed to the first chair at that table. A man was waiting there looking around for someone to date for four minutes. There were two empty seats for females.

Lady Anthea was patting her pearl necklace. She said, "Sue, I don't know that I can do this. Wait, look who's with Mr. Andrews. It's the driving instructor."

I would have to take her word for it since I was back to looking at the rows and rows of hands. "I have to stay." I went to join the waiting man. All because he wore a flannel shirt. And he had hands.

I sat and reached out to shake his hand, and took a closer look at it. "I'm Sue Patrick. You look familiar," I said. His hand, however, didn't look similar to the one that held me down. Which was either good news, or bad.

"I'm Ty, and so do you." His slow smile was intended to be sexy. "I saw you at Buckingham's on Sunday, right?"

"I'm one of the co-owners," I said.

Lady Anthea came and sat down in the empty chair to my right, and looked across the table at someone who looked like a teenager. Surely there was a lower age limit at these things. I was tempted to eavesdrop—because that was going to be good—but I resisted. "At the driving class?" I asked.

"Yeah, but it wasn't much of a class," he said with a lazy laugh. "Now I see that old man with the anger issues and his dog are here." Though he wasn't as old as Charles, he was in his midfifties. Why was *old* always five years older than one's own age?

"You were with Roman Harper?" I asked.

"Yeah, he's a neighbor. He called and wanted to go. The guy's brilliant, has a photographic memory, so you can imagine how the instructor got on his nerves."

The librarian rang a bell and Ty shifted up one chair for his date with Lady Anthea and someone else sat down. He scribbled something on the lined notepaper we'd each been given. "Sue—hot," it read.

The young woman was standing between two tables dealing with an argument between daters on the far end of the middle row. She flapped her arms up and down in an attempt to get the men to lower their voices. When I saw one of the offenders was Charles Andrews, I mentally wished her lots of luck. He didn't want to move to the next seat, and let it be known he would leave the premises rather than conform to such an unreasonable restriction on his liberty.

The driving instructor was in such a state of awe at the man, I thought she would melt. She looked at Charles. "My dating days are over," she cooed. She wore a black silk turtleneck and a skirt that ended an inch below her knees, along with sensible pumps.

He leashed So-Long and put him on the floor, then he and the woman walked between the tables on their way out. She wrapped his right arm in both of hers.

Why was he walking through a group of people with a dog who had been agitated minutes earlier and without the use of both arms? How far would he go to impress her? When I saw the look So-Long gave Ty, I sprang from my chair and ran around the table. A study from about a decade ago reported that one in five Dachshunds had bitten or tried to bite a stranger, with some studies describing them as an aggressive breed. Personally, I like to think of each dog as an individual, and I had to admit this particular one was motivated. Sure, he'd learned crankiness at the feet of a master, and been an apprentice his whole life, but I'd never observed any unprovoked aggressiveness.

No!" I said when I got in front of him. The growl had already started. I snapped my fingers in front of his face. I didn't want to repeat the verbal correction. He slowly took his eyes off Ty's backside and looked at me. We had always gotten along at Buckingham's and he didn't know who would win our staring contest. But I knew. He looked down and I whispered, "Good dog." I moved to the side and let him pass.

As Charles Andrews walked by he glanced at me and quirked the corner of his lip. He kept moving, leading his ladylove out. He had smiled at me. If I didn't know better, I would think he was acknowledging that I had gotten him out of a jam. A normal person wouldn't want his dog to bite anyone, out of concern for the victim. Charles Andrews wasn't normal. He was, however, a retired attorney and therefore well aware of the personal liability he could have from an unprovoked dog attack away from home.

"I hate dogs," Ty was saying to Lady Anthea.

"It appears the feeling is mutual," she responded with a laugh.

I returned to my chair and looked across at my new date—John. "What happened to the guy who was sitting here?"

"He had someplace to go."

Chapter 23

Lady Anthea and I had picked up tacos from Taco Reho, an upscale food truck in the Big Chill Surf Cantina's parking lot, and now we were driving north on Route 1, headed back to my house to get Albert. We were going to Roosevelt Inlet to enjoy our delicacies. The sun would set around seven thirty and we intended to be there to see that it did.

"I'll pick up Abby and check on Marin and then we can go," I said.

"After a full day of bossing that Pekingese around, Abby should be knackered," she said. "And Marin loved every minute of it."

"Shelby said Marin did so much better today than yesterday. There didn't seem to be nearly as much stress."

We took a shortcut through the Arby's parking lot to get to the Villages of Five Points. She looked around and asked, "What is this?"

"They sell roast beef sandwiches. That's why it's *R-B's.*"

"We don't have so many fast-food restaurants in England." She had always been curious about the town and American culture and life in general. Her brother could not have cared less. When we crossed Savannah Road to enter the subdivision she spoke again. "We're all set for the late rehearsal?" she asked.

"So far, so good. I haven't heard from Cordy so I'm assuming the musicians agreed to the plan. I left a check for the room deposit. We need to be there a little before eight, and when we finish, the cleaning crew will lock up," I said. "Will you be able to get away from your brother?"

"I told him we would be cleaning crates," she said with a chuckle. "He didn't offer to join us. Did you tell John about our plan?"

I nodded. "He's not wild about it since the murderer could be someone in the orchestra. He doesn't trust Bess Harper or Cordy Galligan."

"So, as usual, he's jumping to conclusions!"

"He doesn't suspect them of murder—yet—but you have to admit every clue points to the Potomac Symphony Orchestra. And both women have lied to him. Cordy said she never met the first victim but we have a photo of them together the morning of the day he died. Bess Harper said she didn't call the second victim, but her phone says otherwise. It's like because they're in the arts, no one wants to call bullshit."

Lady Anthea pinched the bridge of her nose. "I do want him to find out who killed Georg Nielsen. He was a musical genius."

I hit my steering wheel with my palms in frustration. "And because Nick Knightley was an ex-con, his murder isn't as important?"

"I apologize. You're right, of course. I'm frustrated and annoyed that we're having to spend our time on late-night rehearsals because of my brother when we should be working to solve *both* murders."

I turned onto West Batten. She was convinced that time spent with the PSO was time taken away from the investigation, and I was just as sure of the opposite. Albert would soon be with us so we had a good excuse to drop the subject.

* * * *

Albert had not been able to get comfortable or feel stable in the folding beach chair and kept reminding me of that. Abby had been sitting by my left foot, but stood and moved to my right side to get farther from him as he fidgeted.

"After a certain age, the height of these chairs is much more comfortable than sitting on the ground," I said, trying to make light of his comment.

He went back to his second grievance: handheld food. Never mind that the Taco Reho chef had trained under Thomas Keller, among other luminaries. His third complaint pushed me over the edge. He wanted wine with his dinner—in a wineglass. It seemed common sense would explain why we didn't want *glass,* but it hadn't. I told him that it was illegal to have alcohol on Lewes beach, and that meant from Roosevelt Inlet to the Lewes–Cape May Ferry. I'm not saying my friends would want anyone getting within sniffing distance of our water bottles or soda cans, but we drew the line at open glasses of vino. I had a long night ahead of me, so I hadn't been tempted. Then he complained about the early dinner time, though I told him what time the sun would set. He didn't think to suggest we eat afterward, rather than during, and for that I was grateful since I wanted some time at Buckingham's before going back to the library.

"Albert!" Lady Anthea snapped. "What's really bothering you? Are you worried about the concert?"

He looked down sheepishly. "Do you blame me? Did you see them today? And it got worse after you left!"

"Uh, well, if you would rather not be their guest conductor, I'm sure they would understand," I said.

"They need me! And a gentleman always keeps his word!" His indignation caused the pitch of his voice to rise to a level that made me worry Abby might start to howl.

"What happened?" I asked.

He shook his head. "It was a disgrace. That symphony orchestra is a hotbed of rumors and backbiting."

I thought about how lucky I was to enjoy my life and my work at Buckingham's, which was more than I could say for the musicians in the symphony orchestra. "Rumors? About what?" I asked.

"I don't know, but they were whispering to each other."

I glanced over at Lady Anthea and she looked down at her lap. They were probably whispering about his ineptitude.

"You did volunteer," Anthea reminded him.

"This is taking me away from my true passion," he said with a pout.

"What is it this week?" she asked.

"Participatory art. Yayoi Kusama is a genius. After experiencing her Infinity Mirrors, I understand infinity," he said.

"Speaking of infinity, looks like we're about to have a beautiful sunset," I said, looking around at the water and the sky.

Brother and sister looked out, and at least Lady Anthea appreciated the changing colors of the sky.

I tried again to make nice. "Albert, I am sorry you won't be seeing Georg Nielsen conduct, but at least you'll hear his composition. The bit I heard this morning was…" I couldn't find the word to describe how it had affected me. "Very moving."

"Hmm. I guess."

"Who is *your* favorite composer?" I asked.

"Depends on my mood. Sometimes Rachmaninov. Sometimes Grieg."

Lady Anthea was smiling at us, looking back and forth. "Isn't Grieg sometimes just too-too?" she asked.

I had no idea what that meant, but Albert did. They went on talking about "Lyric Pieces," which I learned were short works written by Grieg. They were in their world and that wasn't my world. Unfortunately, mine included a double murder and an attempt on my life. They went on talking and I sat there half listening. The sun dropped below the horizon and I waited to see if they would notice. They didn't. I stood and gathered the takeaway papers from our dinner. Lady Anthea and Albert took the hint and stood up and folded their chairs.

Suddenly I missed John. Even though I'd seen him at the library, we were again talking at cross-purposes. It seemed like he was never nearby and when he was, he made cryptic comments about the duke.

While we were loading the Jeep, my phone let me know I had a new text. *Worse than I thought,* Mason had written.

* * * *

When Lady Anthea and I dropped Albert off at my neighbor's house and Abby off at home, it was after seven thirty, which meant we wouldn't have time to go to Buckingham's. I texted that news to Mason.

J and I will meet you at Taj Mahal. Our town's new library on Adams Avenue was given this moniker because of its size and formal architectural design.

Around twenty people stood shivering in the portico. Most were dressed in jeans and a sweatshirt or sweater. I recognized the oboist, a couple of the violinists, and the quick-tempered woman who played the triangle. She was wearing a black sweatshirt with the words, *HERE COMES TREBLE.* I remembered how she'd acted during the earlier rehearsal and laughed at the accuracy of the sentiment. Cordy stood near the door and the bus driver hovered nearby. Library patrons were drifting out as closing time neared.

"We're in the large conference room," I told her. "It's on the left."

"I'll direct you," Lady Anthea offered, holding the door open.

"Don't start until eight o'clock," I reminded her.

As my business partner waited by the door, Cordy looked out at the assembled group. When she turned and went inside, they followed. They had been waiting for direction from her. As they filed past me, they didn't look like lemmings, following without thought. They did it because of the special hold she had over them. Where did that power come from? Her talent?

The bus driver sidled in with the group. Margo brought up the rear. I was about to follow her. Since the library would be open a few more minutes, maybe I could check out a book or two. I had finished *A Table Setting for A Slaying.*

"Pssst."

I looked around but there was no one there. With one or two killers on the loose I didn't want to be standing outside in the dark, alone, so I turned to go in.

"Pssst."

"Mason?" I whispered.

"Back here," Joey answered. He and Mason were standing near the curb. Two women and a man exited the library, probably employees or volunteers, and my groomers turned their faces away likes spies in an old movie. When I went to join them, they moved away to stand near a streetlight in the parking lot. I followed, though this was getting a bit cloak-and-dagger, even for me.

Shelby was waiting there, with Bernice.

"What's up?" I whispered.

"Is there anything we need to know about our jobs?" she asked.

I looked around at their faces. It was a serious question. "What are you talking about?"

"The duke thinks you want to marry him."

Chapter 24

"Where would he get such an idea?" I answered my own question. "He has the brains of a dog biscuit, but why would you three think there was a chance in hell that would happen?" I sputtered.

"When I showed him around he acted like he was interviewing me and checking out the Pet Palace to see if it was good enough," Mason said.

"He didn't know about all the awards you've won?" I asked.

"Sue, he thinks you're dying to marry him." Shelby was speaking gently.

I repeated my first question. "Why does he think that?"

Joey spoke up. He's shy and says little, but when he does, it's on the money. "Dana and I—"

"Dana? Isn't she back at school in New York?"

"We thought she needed to be brought in," Mason said. "For her, let's say, special talents."

"Finding stuff on the internet?" I asked.

All three nodded. Bernice probably was too, but it was dark so I couldn't tell.

Joey went on. "Dana and I think that because he's a duke he assumes any woman would want to marry him."

"Why would *he* want to marry me?" I asked. I thought about how he had ignored me since he arrived. Not one of them would meet my eye. "Don't everyone speak at once. This is where you're supposed to say, "Gosh, who wouldn't want to marry a catch like you, Boss!""

Finally Shelby stepped up as the spokesperson. "We've learned more. Dana found where he told a British business group he was coming to the States to increase his financial holdings. You've created a profitable small business. His sister told him about it. He's got to be aware of the money she brings in from her share of the profits and from the classes she gave last year."

"He said he would be increasing their share in Buckingham's," Mason said. "I don't know if he meant by marrying you or by some other means."

The musicians were warming up. Then they were quiet. I hadn't heard the oboist's magic *A* note, so they hadn't tuned.

"I need to talk to Lady Anthea. And I need to get in there."

"Wait," Mason said.

I did wait, though I knew at eight o'clock the doors would be locked.

"I maaaay have painted a less-than-flattering picture of, well, you," he said.

"Do I want to hear this?" I asked.

"High-maintenance, bad temper, abusive to employees, etcetera."

"Good," I said.

"Prison time," Mason went on.

"I don't want to hear any more. Whatever happened to just turning down a marriage proposal?"

"Dana says this way he won't even propose and he'll think twice before he tries anything funny to get a portion of the business."

I looked back at the dark library. "See you in the morning."

"Good night, Sue," Mason said.

"It's Duchess, and don't you forget it."

"LOL," Mason said, giving my shoulder a squeeze.

They left for their cars, relieved their jobs were safe, and I walked back to the library. The door was locked and the inside was dark except for the room on the left side. I pressed my forehead to the glass, looking for someone to let me in. No such luck. I told myself to knock on the door while it was still possible that someone might hear me, but that's not what I wanted to do. Then I heard the note for tuning. I sat down and leaned back against the door.

When I heard the first bars of the 1812 Overture I closed my eyes and imagined myself on my surfboard, being lifted and lowered by waves. There were starts and stops and I imagined Cordy giving instructions in her quiet way.

"'Are You Lonesome Tonight'?" The baritone voice came out of the dark. I opened my eyes. "It's just me," John said.

"How about a different Elvis song? 'Stranger in My Own Home Town'?"

"May I join you?"

"Sure." I patted the concrete. "How long have you been here?"

"Long enough."

The orchestra paused and when they began again, they were on to the new piece.

"Isn't that nice? I guess Georg Nielsen really was a genius," I said.

"So that's *The Ocean, Our Original Opus*?" he said, taking my hand.

"You mean *Symphony by the Sea*?"

Chapter 25

When the concrete became too uncomfortable, John and I sat in the police car. His mobile computer made intimacy a challenge, but we laughed and made the best of it. Since Sunday it had seemed that every time one of us zigged, the other zagged. Now we were close again.

On the way home with Lady Anthea, I couldn't take the smile off my face. "How was the rehearsal?" I asked.

"Cordy was masterful! She knew Georg Nielsen's work like the back of her hand."

"*Symphony by the Sea*?" I asked. She nodded, still dreamy. "Have you seen the sheet music?"

"I peeked at the score and the parts," she said, almost giddy.

"And it was the same piece that they played this morning?" I asked. "After the 1812 Overture?"

"Exactly," she said, then she hummed a few bars of the opening. "They got farther along with it tonight. Lovely and smooth. Well, all but the ending. They stopped before the last movement. They'll rehearse that tomorrow."

"Does the name of a classical music piece ever change?" I asked, not wanting to let the subject go.

"If the composer is alive and makes a revision, it might. Why the interest?"

"I saw the music score on the USB drive and—"

"That would be silly. Why would you have a score on a USB drive?" she asked.

That she would ask *me* was funny. "Is that a rhetorical question?"

"Usually, the conductor tells the concertmaster the right *set* of marks to use on the score. Remember, that's for every instrument needed for the piece. Then Cordy would mark the parts—those are the sheets for each section of the orchestra—for the bowings for the violins. That's who usually has the job. You can hardly do that on a computer, now can you?" Again, rhetorical.

"Isn't there software to write music?"

"Yes, but these marks indicate when the bow goes up and when it's pulled down."

"Could you tell by looking at the USB drive if *Symphony by the Sea* is what they're playing?"

"I think so," she said.

"Let's go to the police station tomorrow after the morning rehearsals," I said as we turned onto Village Main Boulevard from Savannah Road. "How did the musicians seem? It's been a long day for them."

"Some seemed tired by the end, but they'll be fine."

"Elvis performed over seventeen hundred concerts," I said.

"I've missed hearing about your Elvis," she said with a laugh.

We drove through the night and when we reached West Batten, she spoke again. "I have a confession to make."

I realized I was holding my breath, not wanting her to say anything that would hurt our friendship.

"When I saw how distant you treated Chief Turner on Sunday night, I began to harbor a hope that you and my brother could—uh, uh."

"Uh, what?"

"Become a couple."

"I don't think either of us want that," I said tactfully. "And John and I are fine." There. I had said it. And if it made Albert come after Buckingham's, I would fight like a big dog.

Chapter 26

If Tuesday's rehearsal with Albert was a skirmish, Wednesday's was an out-and-out brawl. The furniture had been moved to make room for the musicians and I found a sofa to occupy and stay out of the way of any flying objects. Like, say, a triangle. On the short drive to the community center, Albert was relaxed and pleasant. Lady Anthea had gone next door to talk to him last night. I assumed his change in attitude was because he no longer saw me as a wily hunter with her sights set on a man with a title. Lady Anthea was at Buckingham's greeting pet parents and giving refresher training, gratis. The world was brighter all around.

They played the 1812 Overture, with little enthusiasm. They often talked to one another as they played. This annoyed their neighbors. The offenders' shoulder shrugs said that it didn't matter, but surely they knew the night rehearsals had to be kept secret from Albert.

Cordy was back to calling the new piece *Symphony by the Sea.* While she seemed confident, it was hard going for the others. The first movement was a joy to listen to as the others in the string section watched Cordy's bow with the focus of Labrador Retrievers. In the second movement, trouble erupted in the woodwind section almost immediately. The tempo varied from musician to musician. Some stopped and tried to rejoin. I moved to get a closer look at Albert. He was drawing an *L* in the air, oblivious to what he was causing.

The oboist stopped playing and yelled out, "As it comes, people, as it comes!"

"Look, a slur!" the triangle player yelled, pointing at her music. So many terms for Lady Anthea to define when I saw her again.

Something about this was familiar. They were acting like Charles Andrews, So-Long and the others at the drivers' class on Sunday!

"I meant in the last movement!" the oboist responded.

This time Cordy stood and intervened. "From the beginning of the third movement. Remember it's DEE-pom-pom, not de-POM-POM."

The musicians nodded, understanding her perfectly. Some cleared their throats. They were ready for a fresh start. She sat and raised her violin to her shoulder and nodded once at Albert. This movement reminded me of romance. Then it began to slow, like it was winding down. Albert's shoulders were slumped. The musicians looked at him more and their music less. He was slowing down. The *L*'s he drew stood for languid. His arm was getting tired and the musicians were responding accordingly.

In the last movement, even Cordy seemed down, and I remembered Lady Anthea's comment last night on her difficulty with the ending. Her brow furrowed. Once she glanced up at Albert and remembered there was no help to be had there, the way there would be with a real conductor. She looked at the rest of the orchestra and shook her head. They limped through and finally we were put out of our misery.

Albert shook hands with Cordy. I'd seen this done at concerts but didn't know if it was the tradition for rehearsals. He was smiling. She was smiling.

I met him at the door and we walked to the Jeep,

"I've heard about the outlet stores you have and I'd like to see what they're like," he said.

I wanted to tell him that entire industries had been built on Americans trying to copy the way he and his sister dressed effortlessly, but I figured the irony would be lost on him. "Sure."

* * * *

After a lunch of sandwiches, Lady Anthea, Albert and I went shopping at the outlets on Route 1. He was intrigued by something he saw in the window of Ralph Lauren and we went in.

He led us to a fixture of navy blazers. "Anthea, what coat of arms is this?" he asked.

"It's no one's," I said.

"But here's the coronet," he said.

"It's for marketing. I'm sorry."

He looked at me for elaboration. *Pleeeease drop it.* Maybe I could get him off the subject. "What's a coronet?" I finally said.

"It's similar to a crown, but much smaller. And, of course, only a sovereign can wear a crown."

"Of course."

"The coronet for a duke has eight strawberry leaves and is only worn for coronations."

"And you have one?"

"Yes, I do. Many dukedoms do not because of the cost, and use the image on their coat of arms." I could tell he enjoyed explaining this to me. There would be extraordinary costs involved with this way of life. "I don't know why someone would..." He pointed to the blazer and waited.

I looked to Lady Anthea for help, but she was looking out the store's window. She understood my country's Anglophile tendencies. Hell, we based Buckingham Pet Palace's business theme on it. She was smiling, biting her lower lip, and patting her pearl choker. "Albert, look around. We'll be right back." She pulled my arm and we went outside. "Look!" She pointed to an electric-blue electric car with Virginia license plates. "Call Chief Turner!"

I was already getting my phone out of my handbag, which is really a beach bag. "First I'll take a photo of the tag."

* * * *

Lady Anthea and I sat on a bench, keeping our eyes on the car and waiting for John. A woman, loaded down with shopping bags from Kate Spade and Tory Burch, walked toward the car.

"Cordy Galligan!" I said in disbelief.

"Cordy Galligan!" Lady Anthea said, with disappointment.

She heard us call her name and turned. Then she opened the passenger door, flung her packages in and darted to the driver's side. I stood and held up my phone for her to see. She looked inside the car and then back at me, knowing she had a decision to make. Two police cars turned in, sirens blaring. She hung her head and walked to us.

Chapter 27

"I would like for someone to tell me what this is about," Cordy haughtily demanded of John when he entered the interrogation room and sat at the head of the six-foot table. She had been waiting there with Officer Statler, who had chauffeured her to the Lewes police station, gratis.

Lady Anthea and I were crowded into the tiny viewing cubbyhole for the interrogation room, where we could watch and listen. We had dropped Albert off at his temporary digs and he was enjoying "American telly."

John turned his head and I saw him roll his eyes. "I'm curious. How did your car get to Lewes? Didn't you come in on the bus with the rest of symphony orchestra on Monday?"

From the window we could see her gulp. That was not a question she expected. "Do I need an attorney?"

"I don't know. Do you?" She didn't answer so he asked another. "Do you still claim you never met Georg Nielsen?"

"Tell the truth," I whispered, "before this goes too far."

"I don't believe she had the strength to hold Georg Nielsen under water, any more than Bess, and we know it was a man who killed Nick Knightley," Lady Anthea said.

"If she was driving the getaway car, she's guilty of, uh, what would it be? Conspiracy or something like that?"

Cordy looked up from her lap and spoke. "I knew *of* him."

And I knew what was coming next. John had evidence and was about to use it to catch her in a lie. "You telephoned the victim, Mr. Nielsen, eleven times last week."

She hesitated, startled. Maybe from the look on John's face, she decided to be more forthcoming. "I saw him in New York City on Saturday morning."

"Why?" he asked.

"I just thought since we were going to be performing together, we should meet."

"And you left Virginia to meet with him in Manhattan?"

"Yes, that's where he was," she said.

I shook my head. "She's a really bad liar. I hope she sticks with the violin. Or goes back to it when she gets out of prison."

"Why do you assume she's lying?" Lady Anthea said, looking at me.

"Why would she go all the way to New York City to meet him on Saturday if she was going to see him here two days later?" I offered.

John leaned over the table. "Though you were going to see him on Monday? Seems like a lot of trouble." He waited for her response but there wasn't to be one. "So you and your car were on the ferry with the victim on Saturday evening?"

Cordy nodded.

"And then what happened?"

"He and I went to Lewes Beach and sat and talked. I left him there. Very much alive."

"What time?"

"Around ten o'clock, maybe ten thirty."

"Any witnesses?" he asked.

Cordy shook her head.

"Who is Alexander Whittle?"

"Alex?" she rasped. John nodded. "He's the orchestra's bus driver. He doesn't have anything to do with this."

"You telephoned him late Saturday night and again on Sunday morning. Why?"

I leaned over to Lady Anthea. "He must have gotten her phone records after Dana sent the photo of her with Nielsen." She nodded.

"He works for the PSO," she said, as if that moved things along.

John ran his hand over the top of his head. Cordy Galligan had gone too far. "I have one more question. Who was the man you picked up on Sunday morning on Bayview Avenue?"

"I, I didn't pick anyone up!" she said.

John stood. "I'm placing you under arrest. Maybe your memory will improve." Then he spoke to Officer Statler. "Read her her rights."

Officer Statler rose and motioned for Cordy to get up.

I had typed as fast as I could, but the text message seemed to take forever to arrive. Then as we watched, John took his phone out of his pocket and saw it was from me. He read it and turned so I could see the side of his face. He hadn't understood the message, and his look said *This better be good.*

"Ms. Galligan, who did you board your dog with on Saturday night?"

"All right, I'll tell you what you want to know," she said.

All three sat back down.

"How did you get back to Virginia?" he asked.

"I called Alex and he came." Her voice had softened around the phrase *and he came.*

"Where did he meet you?"

"In the Home Depot parking lot."

"What time did he get to Lewes?"

She looked at her hands, completely still, on the table. I had the impression she could sit there forever and not speak. I was wrong. John moved his chair back and that was all it took.

"Sometime in the late morning. I'm not sure."

"I think she's telling the truth. All he has to do is look at the store's security camera footage and he can verify it," Lady Anthea whispered.

"Yeah, it sounds true. After all, she was still in Lewes in the morning since that's when she picked the man up. Makes sense," I said.

John was speaking, "I'm going to release you on your own recognizance. I don't think you're a flight risk. I think you enjoy your position with the PSO and your reputation too much to put them in jeopardy. We've impounded your car. You're not to leave town."

He told the recorder the session was ending. Officer Statler walked out with Cordy. John followed them.

Lady Anthea said, "I'd rather Cordy not know we were here. She might feel uncomfortable. Can we give her time to leave?"

"She might need a ride," I said. "Or I guess she could just walk to the hotel." I had to stop rambling and say what was on my mind. "Lady Anthea, she might have a more serious problem than being embarrassed."

I texted John. *Is she gone?*

Coast is clear. He rapped on the door. It was just two quick knocks but we jumped.

Lady Anthea was closest and she opened it. "You startled us."

"Were you standing out here?" I asked. "How long were you going to leave us in there?"

He stood to the side and we walked out. "I had to tell someone to go pick up Alex Whittle."

"Why didn't you tell me what you saw on the traffic cameras on Sunday morning?" I asked. He started to answer but I stopped him. "You've known all week she was the one driving that car!"

Chapter 28

"Chief?" Officer Statler stood in the doorway to the city hall building that housed the police station.

John and I stood outside and Lady Anthea chose to wander off rather than listen to us argue. "Who was in the car with her?" I asked.

"Chief?" Officer Statler could be a very determined woman.

Finally he pulled his eyes off me and turned to her. "Yes?"

"The dispatcher has Alexander Whittle on the phone. She transferred him to the nonemergency line. It's patched through," she said as she handed him a phone.

I waved at Lady Anthea and my excitement brought her back. "Did you hear that?" I kept my voice down so Mr. Whittle wouldn't hear. "The bus driver is calling. Cordy must have told him he was going to be brought in for questioning. Finally, we're making progress!"

"Do you mind if I ask why you want her present?" John asked.

"Is he lawyering up?" I whispered to Officer Statler. She shrugged.

"Because of how she feels about music. I see," John said. "She's here and I'll ask her now."

"Music?" Lady Anthea asked. "Of course, I'll sit in on his interview."

"Uh, actually he wants Sue there," John said, apologetically.

She stared at me in disbelief. I nodded that I would be happy to stay and John passed that along. Next, he told Statler to notify the two officers who had gone to bring the orchestra's bus driver in that he would be coming under his own steam.

"Maybe he's in the Elvis army," John said. I took their kidding and thought about how Alex Whittle had looked at me when he saw the solace I'd felt from *Symphony by the Sea*.

"Chief Turner, I'm concerned about my brother being around the orchestra and their staff. Was this the man Cordy picked up?"

"No," I interrupted. "I've seen his hands and he wasn't the man who attacked me."

John exhaled a long breath. "Sue, I know you don't want to hear this again, but you can't count on your memory for what the hand looked like. Especially since you saw it under water." He hesitated before he went on. "From the footage it looks like she was alone in the car."

"Could whoever it was have been hiding, maybe on the car's floor?" I asked.

He shook his head. "The car was too small."

"Like in our last case? Remember Rick's father's clown car?" I asked.

"Was not *our* case."

"You're such a stickler but, fine, *my* case," I said. "But mi case is su case. Damn it." They looked at me like I had really cussed. "We're not hitting dead ends. We're hitting brick walls and every single time it's because of the PSO." John stared at me but didn't bother to correct my pronoun again.

"How is Rick?" Lady Anthea asked. Had she changed the subject because I had criticized her precious classical musicians? He was the owner of Raw-k & Roll. She had met him on her first visit and gotten to know him better during the second when we cleared his father of a murder charge.

"I'll see him at Cape Henlopen later this afternoon," I said as we walked into the hallway.

"Are you going surfing?" John asked.

"SUPing." Though he had yet to join me, he knew that was the acronym for stand up paddle boarding. It was Wednesday and I hadn't been on the water since Saturday. "Would you mind if Lady Anthea looked at the music score on that USB drive?"

"Sure, but why?" he asked.

"We want to be certain that's the piece the orchestra is rehearsing this week," she answered.

"Does it really matter what they're playing?" John asked.

The truth was, I had no idea if it mattered, but the fact that Georg Nielsen's masterpiece—the one that was supposed to catapult him from prodigy conductor to prodigy composer—had two titles bothered me. Was it too much to hope it might be a loose brick?

I turned to see the bus driver walking in, so we didn't have to answer.

Alexander Whittle ambled up to John. He didn't appear nervous and he was in no hurry to get there.

"Thank you for coming in," John said. He spoke to people with true respect. "We'll go in here." He opened the door to the interrogation room and Whittle went in.

We sat around the table and once the recorder was on, John listed our names.

"Please tell us about your whereabouts and activities this past Saturday night," he began.

John had posed the question, but Whittle looked at me when he answered. "I was with my wife, my kids and my in-laws. It was my wife's birthday party." He pulled out his phone and swiped the screen. "I'll show you the photographs of the party."

"That won't be necessary. What time did you get home?" John said.

I reached for the phone and looked at the photos. "I hope you can come back to Lewes and bring your family. We have a new bowling alley."

John cleared his throat.

"We got home around nine o'clock. Ms. Galligan called me at about ten thirty. She was upset. She said she was in Lewes. I—"

"What *exactly* did she say when she called?" John interrupted.

"Nothing that had to do with these murders," he said, again addressing me.

"Can you remember what she said?"

Whittle answered, but reluctantly. "She said 'it's not fair,' but she never said *what* wasn't fair."

"Did you ask her?" John asked.

At first Whittle's furrowed brow had me thinking he didn't understand what he was being asked. I put his hesitancy in answering the last few questions together with my images of him when I'd observed him in Cordy's presence and felt I understood. He held her in such deference that he felt these questions impertinent.

"And then what happened?"

"She said she was all right where she was and we hung up."

"Where *was* she?" I asked.

Whittle shook his head. "I don't know."

"Was she indoors or outside? Could you hear the ocean? Was she in her car?" I asked.

"No, she was indoors. That's how it sounded." That elaboration, that added-on phrase, told me, told all of us, that he was withholding information.

"She's famous," I said slowly. "Could she have a fan who would do something like this? Kill two people?"

"Two people? Didn't Nick Knightley kill Maestro Nielson?" he asked.

"We don't know yet," John said. "What happened next?" By that he meant, *I know what happened next.*

"She called again the next morning. She was more upset, too upset to drive, so I came to get her and take her to her home."

"Where do you live?" John asked, again a question to which he surely already knew the answer.

"Hyattsville, Maryland," he said. His hands were clasped on the table and I studied them. Those were not the hands that had held me under water and made me think I was dying. He caught me staring. "I didn't kill anybody."

"I know." I was whispering, and I hadn't meant for my voice to come out like that.

"Thank you for letting Ms. Galligan go," he said.

I knew John was going to give me a hard time later for Alexander thanking *me* for Cordy's freedom. I smiled and pointed to John. "Thank him." Then I leaned closer. "You know at some point someone is going to have to, uh, be honest. You're going to have to stop *protecting* each other and tell Chief Turner what happened." I straightened and tried to lighten the mood. "After all, you have a concert coming up."

His expression, of wariness and wanting so badly to be understood, didn't change. "It's the music."

"I don't understand," John said.

"The music has to be protected. Cordy didn't kill anyone. Please don't upset her. She *makes* music."

The emphasis he'd placed on *makes* told me he didn't mean in the everyday sense. "When she plays the violin?" Lady Anthea asked. "She's masterful."

Alexander Whittle shook his head. "She *makes* music," he repeated. "It's nothing when it's just the score. That's just paper." I wondered if a composer would agree, but that would be a question for Lady Anthea. "When music is *heard*, it's created."

I pulled out my phone. "Sorry, I have to check this," I lied. Then I texted Margo Bardot. *Alexander Whittle being taken into custody.* I pushed my chair back and smiled.

Chapter 29

Lady Anthea, Chief Turner and I stood in his office. He was too mad to sit so the two of us stood in the doorway and Lady Anthea stood next to his desk. "You terminated my interview!" he bellowed.

"I had to," I said.

"Why?"

"Because Cordy will be here in a few minutes," I answered. Of course, my volume was about half of his. "If I'm going to Cape Henlopen we're going to have to speed this up. Plus we have tonight's rehearsal. You can let him go after she leaves."

"I can? Gee, thanks. I haven't made that decision yet. I'm having his location confirmed at the time of each of the phone calls. If they check out, he has an alibi for the time of both murders. I could charge him with obstruction. Or that darling of all prosecutors, conspiracy. Did she tell you she was coming back?"

I glanced back at Lady Anthea, who was slyly reading something on John's desk. That would pay him back for not telling us he had known all week that she was the driver of the electric-blue electric car.

"Not exactly." I told them about my text. "He's obsessed with Cordy. He confuses her with her music. It's like for him the two are the same."

Lady Anthea was nodding. "Sue, you're on to something. You heard him say it, he doesn't see himself as protecting her—he's protecting the music."

"So you're hoping she'll charge down here if she thinks he's being arrested and finally tell us the truth? Okay, not bad," John admitted, grudgingly.

Lady Anthea twisted her pearls. "Did you think he was romantically involved with Cordy?"

"Nah," I said, then I looked at John. "You're sure Cordy does not have the strength to hold Georg Nielsen down to drown him?"

"What do you want me to do? Arm-wrestle her?"

Lady Anthea cracked up.

Traitor, the look I shot her practically said. "Why did she place that first call to Mr. Whittle?" I asked, pretending to ignore him. "You would be that upset if you had just killed a man."

"What possible motive would she have?" Lady Anthea asked, still protecting the concertmaster.

"Here she comes. Let's ask her," John said, gesturing toward the door. "We'll talk to her in here." He walked to meet Cordy and escorted her back to his office, where Lady Anthea and I stood waiting. John sat in his desk chair. Cordy and Lady Anthea took the leather-upholstered guest chairs. I leaned against the wall.

"Are you here to tell us why you telephoned Mr. Whittle on Saturday night?" Chief Turner asked.

"I had been drinking. By then, for many hours," she answered.

I shook my head and John saw that I wasn't buying it. He gave me a *go-ahead* look. So I did. "You spent twelve hours with someone out of—what, professional courtesy?" She tried to say something and I held up my hand. "Let me stop you there. Why do you refer to Nielsen's composition by a different name than everyone else does?"

Cordy's head snapped up to look at me but she didn't speak. If the look in her eyes was any indication, she was too angry to talk.

I pressed on. "At the press conference Margo used the title *Symphony by the Sea,* but at the first rehearsal you called it *The Ocean, Our Original Opus.* The music was kept a secret before its debut. The score and parts you and the rest of the PSO are using says the title of Nielsen's piece is *Symphony by the Sea.*"

She jumped up from her chair like she was going to charge me but John was standing in front of her, menacing, so fast it seemed he had materialized onto the spot.

"It was never Georg Nielsen's composition and it was never called *Symphony by the Sea!*"

"How did you know its original title?" I asked.

"Because I wrote it!"

Chapter 30

Someone in that orchestra had finally spoken the truth.

Cordy took a deep breath. This act of unburdening herself had acted as a balm and her words tumbled out. When she got the sheet music to practice she saw it was her composition. She needed it back. And she needed Georg to admit she was the composer before he performed it, or it would always be seen as his.

After all the talking, she seemed spent from emotion.

"You have been carrying around a heavy burden," Lady Anthea said, kindly.

Cordy nodded and slumped back down onto the chair.

"Let's go over what happened on Saturday night and Sunday morning again," John said.

"And then you'll let Alex go?" she asked.

"Probably."

Cordy hesitated. I saw the look on John's face and I wanted to tell her that was the best deal she was going to get. "Okay. Like I said, I met Maestro Nielsen in New York and we had brunch. I told him that I knew he was passing my composition off as his and that I wanted him to admit it was mine. He acted like he was considering it, so when he asked me to give him a ride to Lewes I said yes. I even suggested the ferry. He drank a lot in the bar on the way over from Cape May. He still hadn't committed, so when we got here, and he wanted to sit on the beach and talk, I said I would. I tried to reason with him, telling him his reputation would suffer, too, when I made all this public. He just laughed at me. I got mad and left."

"Where did you go?" John asked.

"My car. I called Alex. I fell asleep and when I woke up, I drove off."

"You told Mr. Whittle all this?" he asked.

"Sure. He was so sweet," Cordy said, with no idea she'd just outed him as a major liar on her behalf.

"How did Georg Nielsen get it?" I asked, praying that wasn't a dumb question. I had no idea how hard or easy it would have been for Nielsen to get his paws on brand-new sheet music.

"I don't know," she said. "He acted like he was about to tell me. Then he passed out or fell asleep or something. Believe me, he was alive when I left him on the beach." She turned in her chair to face Lady Anthea. "You understand, don't you? He had to admit it was mine before it was performed. If Nick Knightley hadn't killed him, maybe he would have!" As she spoke to Lady Anthea, something over my business partner's shoulder caught her eye and she stopped.

Alex Whittle was walking through the lobby, led by Officer Statler. I watched the scene play out. I imagined Cordy's voice traveling in slo-mo to him. He turned and their eyes met. That part I didn't imagine. He kept walking. Cordy stood and announced, "I drove to the parking lot and slept for a while and in the morning I telephoned Alex and he came for me. That's all I can tell you." I assumed by that she meant it was all she was *going* to tell. That would change once she was arrested.

She walked to the door and only turned around at John's baritone voice. "Remember what I said about staying in town."

"I do remember. Now I have a rehearsal to get ready for." She looked at me and then at Lady Anthea. "Neither of you are welcome there." She marched out as if she thought she was holding all the cards.

We watched her go and finally I spoke. "I honestly don't know how to feel about that."

"Lady Anthea, you're probably more torn up, right?" John said with a kind smile.

If he had suspected her attempted matchmaking, all was forgiven and that made me smile. It also freed up my brain to go back over what Cordy had said. "Assuming she was telling the truth about sleeping in her car, where was she parked? She told that two ways. First that she slept where she was parked, and the second time in the Home Depot parking lot."

"I'll check the cameras, but it wasn't at the beach. We don't allow that. If we didn't patrol, the neighbors would probably report it, anyway."

I laughed. "Neighbors like Bess and Roman Harper would, I bet."

Lady Anthea hadn't spoken for a few minutes. Now she exploded. "Oooooh, I want to *shake* her." She was fuming.

"I don't think I've ever seen you so mad," I said.

"I am angry!" She turned to face John. "Sue and my brother are in danger until we know who Cordy picked up on Sunday morning!"

"I am doing all I can," John said to her, but looking at me.

I nodded to show him I knew he was. He smiled.

She was pacing back and forth in front of his desk now. "They are supposed to be an *orchestra,* not a conspiracy."

"Sue, I keep thinking about what you said about hitting a brick wall named Potomac Symphony Orchestra. It's true," John said. "Any Elvis wisdom?"

"'All Shook Up?'"

"What?" Lady Anthea asked.

"How does that help?" John asked.

"We need to shake them up and see if anyone will turn on the others," I said. "They fight like the proverbial cats and dogs in rehearsal." Then I remembered John hadn't been present at any of these brawls and recounted a few of the highlights. "You should see them."

"So you're suggesting we un-orchestrate the orchestra?" Lady Anthea's raised eyebrow told me she found this interesting.

"Yes, I am."

"When Cordy is in charge she makes them behave," Lady Anthea said.

"Can she control them after they get really out of control?" I wondered.

"How? You two are banned from tonight's rehearsal."

Lady Anthea and I looked at him. She went back to pacing.

"We need to do something about that," I said. "I've got it! I know two people who are not banned from the library. Almost, but not quite. I'll call on Charles Andrews and his new lady. He owes me one for bringing So-Long under control on Tuesday."

"And remember the uproar he created on Sunday at the senior drivers' class?" Lady Anthea said.

"I cannot think of any two people more qualified, with the obvious exception of ourselves. Let's go set it up," she said as we walked out.

"I'll give you a couple of days, but then I will arrest Ms. Galligan," John said.

"Fair," I said.

Lady Anthea glanced back at John. "And Sue, don't forget we're taking *Albert* to dinner tonight."

John's face drooped and he looked at me. Before I followed her out I kissed him. Lips. Hard. Long.

She and I didn't talk as we walked to the Jeep, but when we got inside I said, "I really thought you had given up on that pipe dream of yours for your brother and me to get together, but maybe not. Please do."

"You would be perfect for him. He told me he thinks you're beautiful. You would love Frithsden."

"But John…" Any of the possible ways for me to finish that sentence needed to be spoken to him first.

"He's leaving Lewes," she said.

"No, he's not. He would have told me."

"He applied for the position of assistant police chief of San Francisco. He meets the qualifications and has been chosen along with other qualified applicants to come for an in-person interview." She spoke like she had memorized the lines.

"Where did you get all that?" I felt numb.

"I read a letter on his desk."

Chapter 31

"Let's see, what can Mr. Andrews do to un-orchestrate the orchestra?" Lady Anthea asked.

"I have an idea." I had hatched it before she'd dropped the bombshell about John leaving Lewes.

I was about to telephone Charles Andrews when I saw Rick's text. I had arranged to meet him, along with Charlie and her husband, Jerry, at the water. This Charlie was a very nice person, the opposite of Charles. I hoped he wasn't canceling. Only the ocean could save me now.

Kayak to HOR light instead of SUP? he'd written. I exhaled in relief.

This sounded even better and I would have texted him so, but my time was not my own. Instead I telephoned Charles Andrews. I leaned a little toward the dash like he was under the hood. "How would you like to attend a free dress rehearsal for the Potomac Symphony Orchestra tonight?"

"Wait," he said, straight and to the point. I heard him talking to someone in a much warmer tone than he'd used with me. "Yeah. Where and what time?" By that he had meant, "Thank you and we'd love to take you up on your generous offer."

"At the Lewes Library in the large conference room. Be there by eight o'clock."

Lady Anthea had been motioning that she wanted to say something to Charles. "Mr. Andrews, this is Anthea Fitzwalter. They want this to be a simulation of Friday's concert, so please remember to chat up your friend during the performance. You might even pretend not to pay attention to the musicians. Good evening."

I disconnected the call. "Nice touch," I said. Next I called Jane and Michael Burke from the *Southern Delaware Daily* and extended the same invitation.

"May we bring a couple of our interns along?" Jane asked.

"The more the merrier," Lady Anthea said.

* * * *

"How hard would it be to get our SCUBA certification?" Rick was asking. His ponytail hung down his back. His kayak was yellow, as was his life vest.

We'd talked about learning to dive for months, but since usually there was an adult beverage, usually an Orange Crush, in our hands at the time we never got very far. Certainly not beyond the talking stage. Rick was anxious to explore one of Delaware's artificial reef sites. There were fourteen in the Delaware Bay and down the coast of the Atlantic Ocean. We were specifically interested in the Del-Jersey-Land Inshore artificial reef, which was equidistant from Lewes, Delaware, Cape May, Maryland, and Ocean City, Maryland. Last summer, a forty-three-year-old vessel from the Lewes–Cape May Ferry, the *MV Twin Capes*, was sunk at the site. She joined two other vessels. One was a harbor tug, the *Tamaroa*. In her early days she'd been at the Battle of Iwo Jima and later found fame as the rescue vessel in the book *The Perfect Storm*. Within a week, recreational divers had begun exploring the *MV Twin Capes*.

"You think Dayle might take the classes, too?" Charlie asked from her green kayak. Jerry's kayak matched hers. My tandem kayak was red, and Abby sat up front, wearing her red life vest.

"Hell, I don't know if she'll even let *me*," Rick said.

"Dude, take a stand," Jerry yelled from his kayak. We were paddling around the older, shorter breakwater and the red East End Lighthouse. The water was slightly choppier and slapped against the stones so we had to speak louder to be heard. He popped the top of a can of Dogfish Head 90 Minute IPA, because why not.

"I figure after we get married I can take a stand on things like that," Rick yelled back.

"Women like for men to take a stand," Jerry said.

"No, we don't," Charlie and I said at the same time.

"Rick, when do you think you'll get married?" Charlie called out. She paddled closer to her husband and he handed her the beer. She took a drink and handed it back.

"Soon as she'll have me," Rick said. "She wanted to wait 'til she was through with chemo." He looked out at the horizon and ground his jaw. "She's done with it now, but that was a rough time." He paused, then said, "Sue, you sure are quiet today. You okay?"

I had been enjoying listening to them and I was imagining that the rise and fall of the water under my kayak was taking my troubles and sending them to the bottom of the ocean. All three people waited for my answer. "Well, the murderer, someone who killed twice, might still be in town—"

Rick interrupted me. "Twice? I thought that Knightley guy killed the conductor."

"That's bullshit!" I said, not really knowing where that level of emotion had come from. Abby turned her head around to look at me. "Who's been saying that?"

"I don't know any of their names, but it was someone from that symphony orchestra," he said.

"Nick Knightley wasn't in town at the time of Georg Nielsen's death," I said. "Every time I hear the theory that he killed Nielsen it's been from someone with the PSO."

"Framing the dead guy? That's convenient, isn't it?" Charlie said with a snort.

"Do you have another one of those?" I asked as I paddled closer to Jerry.

He opened one and they passed it to me. I told them about Albert thinking he could conduct, and about the mission Charles Andrews would go on later.

"The guy with the Dachshunds?" Rick asked and I nodded. He knew a number of my pet parents as the supplier of their dogs' superexpensive cuisine.

"Do you know him?" I asked. "Neither So-Long nor So-Lo are on a raw food diet."

Rick chuckled. "Only by reputation, and it is *some* reputation."

"What's Chief Turner going to do?" Jerry asked.

"Call him John," I said.

"Calling law enforcement by a first name? I just can't do it," he said.

Charlie agreed. "That'd be like calling your doctor by his first name. You need a buffer. Now, if you marry him, we'll reconsider."

I shook my head and looked at the sky.

"Is he close to an arrest?" Jerry asked.

"Progress has been slow. That's the reason for tonight's shake-up. The old *John* would have locked up the whole group."

The light and the air around us were changing and the sun would soon set, so without even discussing it, we began paddling to shore instead of going on to the Harbor of Refuge Lighthouse.

Chapter 32

My kayak was on the roof of the Jeep, and Abby was secure in her harness in the back seat. I checked my messages before heading back to Buckingham's. Shelby, Lady Anthea and John all wanted me to call them. "Abby, who should I call first? You're right. I'll call Shelby first since that might be business-related."

"Hi, what's up? My time on the water has hit my reset button."

"Don't come back to Buckingham's tonight," Shelby whispered. "Margo and Bess want to talk to you. They came in around four and I told them you weren't here. They said it was about, quote, "This murder business." They want you to talk to Chief Turner about Nick Knightley killing Georg Nielsen. They left, then Bess came back around five."

I laughed. "Since he already knows Nick Knightley wasn't in town then, I can't convince him otherwise—if I wanted to, which I don't."

"Actually, that's what Bess wanted at first. She changed her mind. Now she wants you to use your influence to clear him. She said Margo felt the same. I bet there is quite a story behind that."

I could feel my shoulders clenching, thanks to the tension that was rushing back into my life. I started the engine and pulled out. "I'm parked at Lewes Beach. I've got to get out of here before Bess sees me from her balcony. We really need a spy at tonight's library rehearsal in case one of them says something about this."

"We're ahead of you. Mason and Joey are going," she said.

"Thank you! And thank them for me! Now I have to call Lady Anthea and John."

"Lady Anthea wants to tell her brother about the dual rehearsals," she said.

"Wonder why? Won't that hurt his feelings?" I asked.

"Yeah, and I thought that was the whole idea of having them under cover of darkness," she said with a laugh.

"I'll see her at home and I'll call John next."

"Get some rest!" she said as we hung up.

I called John as we drove up Savannah Road. He answered on the first ring, which was right after I had turned in the back entrance to my neighborhood.

"I thought I would let you know there's going to be a memorial service for Nick Knightley tomorrow. His parole officer is arranging it." So much for conversational niceties. He had jumped right in with the reason for the call.

"He must have cared about him," I said. "That's nice. It'll be in DC?"

"No, here at St. Peter's, at eleven o'clock."

"Was he from here, or does he have relatives in the area?" I asked.

"He was going to have it in DC, but there wasn't anyone there to come to it. Someone from the symphony orchestra called to ask him about the arrangements and when he told her that, she asked if it could be held here so the musicians could attend."

"You're kidding me!" I yelled. "I thought everyone but Bess was accusing him of a murder he didn't commit."

"When did Bess change her mind?"

I told him about Bess and Margo's difference of opinion, as I'd heard it from Shelby. He didn't say anything at first and I imagined him rubbing his forehead, thinking. Then he said, "I can't come up with a reason for them to care. Are they covering up for someone? Why try to make me think there were two murderers rather than one? To make Knightley's murderer—your attacker—look better? Like he killed one person instead of two? Doesn't help him much."

"Was it Bess or Margo who called his parole officer?" I asked. I was in my driveway and Abby wanted to know why we were just sitting there.

"No, it was Beaut Richards-Tinsman."

"Whaaat kind of a name is that? Please tell me Beaut's a nickname," I said, laughing so hard I was crying.

"Please tell me she didn't give it to herself," John said. He waited a beat before saying, "Sue, I miss you."

"Me, too." I wanted to ask why he wanted to leave Lewes, but I could see Lady Anthea coming out my neighbor's front door. John and I had so much to say to each other. I wanted time and I wanted it to be in person. "So, who is Beaut?"

"She plays the triangle in the orchestra."

"Oooooh. Remember we told you how the symphony orchestra fought each other Tuesday and Wednesday mornings? She was in the middle of both! By the way, Mason and Joey are going to listen in on tonight's rehearsal," I said.

"About that... Like you said, everything we learn leads back to that symphony orchestra. I'm sending Officer Statler to listen in, too."

"Sue?" Lady Anthea was calling to me. I rolled the window down. "Albert will be over at seven."

I looked at my screen. John had hung up.

Chapter 33

I drove into the garage, unhooked Abby from her harness and we went inside.

"Lady Anthea, you do know I was serious that I can only be friends with Albert, right?"

"Oh, yes! I'm resigned to that. But can you blame me for wanting you to do for Frithsden what you did for Buckingham's?"

"Lewes is my home," I said. After my years of traveling around and living in one beach town after another, I liked the sound of that.

"And I know it's none of my business, but I don't want you to be hurt when Chief Turner leaves Lewes for a larger city."

"You don't need my help with Frithsden. From the photos I've seen you're restoring it beautifully."

I fed Abby, and she curled up in the family room with her back wedged against the sofa and went to sleep.

"Wine or gin and tonic?" I asked.

"G&T, but I'll make it."

It was too chilly to sit on the porch so we joined Abby in the family room. I curled up on the sofa and Lady Anthea sat in her favorite overstuffed armchair across from me.

"I'd like to tell Albert about the shadow rehearsals." I opened my mouth to interrupt but she kept going. "I know, I know. We set them up because his sessions were worse than worthless. I'll tell him that it's because the musicians needed more rehearsal time."

"Like it's their fault?" I asked.

"Exactly," she said, nodding. "I'd like to do it tonight and get it over with."

"Good idea. I need to stay inside, anyway," I said.

"To avoid Bess and Margo?"

I nodded. My phone told me I had a text. "This is from Mason. He says that when they get to the library they'll call us so we can hear everything. And they'll mute us." I texted a thumbs-up back to him. "We need to bring Albert up to speed before eight o'clock."

"I wonder if John would like to join us to listen in?" she said. I appreciated the gesture, which was a concession.

I smiled. "I'll call and ask him."

* * * *

Not only did John come for the show, Shelby came too. Both had arrived in time for Grottos Pizza. My cell phone was one-hundred percent charged and on the coffee table waiting for Mason's call.

"It's like the telly hasn't yet been invented and we're sitting 'round the radio," Albert said. His good mood told me he had taken the news of the shadow rehearsals just as his sister intended.

He was parked in one sea-motif upholstered armchair, and Lady Anthea in the other. John was next to me on the matching couch and Shelby was next to him.

John speed-dialed a number, then tucked his phone under his chin. "I need to check in with Statler." He untucked it. "What's going on down there? Are you in place?" Then he said, "Let me know if you hear anything," and hung up. "She's standing in the lobby outside the meeting room. We said we were supplying security since it was after-hours. Filling up the room with observers made Cordy mad, and it seems to have rubbed off on the others."

"I have a text from Joey," Shelby said. "He says, 'They're fighting over a classical music joke. Haven't started rehearsal.'"

"Who fights over a joke?" I asked.

A minute later Shelby read, "Someone complained because it was such an old joke."

"Ask him to tell us the joke." Albert had said more tonight than in the days since his arrival.

As Shelby typed to Joey, my phone rang. Mason was the caller so I answered it, pressed mute, and put it back on the coffee table. We all leaned in only to hear a cacophony. I picked up one voice for a few words, just to lose it when another voice came closer to the phone. Occasionally a note of music would be played and the triangle clanked at regular intervals. I was left once again wondering why Cordy didn't put a stop to it.

"Shelby, ask Joey if Bess and Margo are there," I said.

"Here's the joke. How does a conductor play chicken with the orchestra?" Shelby read, before typing my question.

Lady Anthea and Albert turned to face each other. "Haydn, Symphony 83, *The Hen*!" they said at the same time, and laughed loudly, completely in their element.

John, Shelby and I looked at one another, not exactly in hysterics.

"Bess and Margo are there," Shelby reported.

The sounds in the library meeting room were dampened. Mason was on the move. Next we heard Margo's voice. "Bess," she hissed, "don't blame this on me."

"Why not? You hired the ex-con," Bess said.

"That's confidential information! But if your husband hadn't talked me into hiring Nick Knightley, ye-e-e-e-s an ex-con, we wouldn't be in this mess. 'He's such a music lover,' he kept saying. He was a flatterer. He thought Roman was a god."

The huffing coming over the line told me Bess was doing her breathing exercises. "A lot of young people in IT think that." Calmer, she whispered, "I guess you're right. Maestro Nielsen would still be alive if Nick Knightley hadn't been brought on board."

"Wait, now you think Nick *did* kill Georg?" Margo asked in a breathy murmur.

"I don't know. Roman says I should say I think it was someone else." She sighed. "You know, for the PSO's reputation. Do *you* think he's innocent?"

"No, I just said that because it makes me look incompetent to hire someone who would kill one of the world's most-loved conductors. Wait, Cordy's starting. Let's go back in."

John leaned his head back and looked at the ceiling. "Is there always a self-serving motive for these people?"

"I know," I said. "Whatever happened to the truth?" I was whispering like I didn't get the concept of mute.

He put his arm around the back of the sofa over my shoulders. "This disruption scheme of yours might just work."

The board chair and the executive director were talking again. "How does Cordy seem to you?" Margo asked. "She seems a little distracted to me."

"She'll be fine!" Bess said. "She's tougher than she looks. Last summer her laptop was infected with ransomware. She came to talk to Roman to see if he could unlock it. He spent hours on it but he still couldn't recover her files. She refused to pay! She stood her ground! I saw then what a strong person she is."

The sound of instruments being tuned, chairs sliding, then two quick taps told us the rehearsal was beginning in earnest. In the silent seconds that followed—both here in my house and in the library meeting room—I imagined Cordy's lifted arms. Would the feelings summoned be as intense as when I was there in person? I smiled and waited, hardly breathing. Next she would lower them and we would hear magic.

"Excuse me," Charles Andrews yelled.

"Ohhhh," Cordy moaned.

"I was just wondering—" he began.

The triangle sounded, and it was going like crazy. "This is not a Q and A session!"

Charles was at his annoying best. "I just wanted to ask—"

The triangle cut him off.

A new voice joined in. "Why can't he ask a—"

"That was the driving instructor," Shelby said.

The triangle.

Shelby laughed first. Then Lady Anthea and Albert lost control. They wiped their eyes, again just alike.

"Ring that thing again and I'm coming down there!" I yelled at the phone. I leaned forward to stand, but I was laughing too hard to get up.

"I could have Officer Statler arrest—" John was laughing too hard to finish his sentence.

The next contretemps resulted from the oboist catching a reporter taking notes. Finally, they began and even made it to the end of the 1812 Overture. Cordy magnanimously gave them a five-minute break.

"What are *we* doing? It's like she gave us a break, too," I said. Every one of us in my family room had stood and stretched or moved about, such is the power of suggestion.

"I don't guess we're going to hear anything useful," Lady Anthea said, "but the efforts to disrupt seem very successful."

"I agree," Albert said. "It's just a matter of time before someone breaks ranks."

John reached for my elbow. "I'm going to have to go."

"Listen to this," Shelby said. "It's a text from Joey. *The triangle player was in love with Nick Knightley. They were engaged to get married.*"

"Hmm," Lady Anthea said, nodding.

"We have our weak link," John said. "I'll talk to her tomorrow." I walked him to the door and we stood there.

"I was thinking about what you said about self-serving motives," I said. "A motive to say someone was innocent when you didn't think so, would be to keep him from being checked out. Right?"

"To stop anyone from looking too closely? We already know he was in prison." He leaned over and kissed me sweetly on my forehead. "Okay. I'll be talking to his parole officer in the morning when he comes for the memorial service and I'll try to learn more. Maybe between him and the triangle player I'll get a more complete picture. Now, I have to get back to the station."

I reached for his arm to stop him from leaving. "You like Lewes, don't you?"

"You're here," he said, leaning over me.

"Other than that? Do you like the town?"

"Better than I thought I would," he said. "Why these questions?"

I reached up and closed the gap between our faces so we could properly kiss.

Chapter 34

"Before he got the job at the symphony the guy couldn't tell a tuba from a trombone, but he sure did love listening to classical music," Nick Knightley's parole officer, Jake Granger, said, his Southern accent emphasizing the vowels in almost every word. The slightly built African-American man looked close to retirement age, but he wasn't phoning it in. I liked him immediately because he had cared about his charge. "And smart as a whip. Just think, he was finally using that brainpower to get ahead." He motioned to John, who was standing next to him, with his thumb. "I was telling the chief that I used to tell him he used his intelligence to be stupid."

Lady Anthea and I had been standing on the porch of St. Peter's Church, next to red doors propped open for the eleven o'clock memorial service, when they walked up and John had introduced us.

"I guess you'd have to be smart and stupid in equal measure to know how to commit internet fraud, but not how to keep from getting caught," John said.

"What kind of scam was it?" I said.

"Ransomware, if you can believe that," Granger said.

"We can believe it," I said.

"We can?" John looked at me, squinting in befuddlement. The simple facial expression and simpler question brought a smile to Jake's face.

He looked from John to me and chuckled. "So that's how it is." We were just that obvious.

I looked around to be sure no one could hear us. "That's what happened to Cordy's computer last year."

"But he only started the job with the symphony orchestra, what, five months ago?" the parole officer said.

"This is what I meant by the Gordian knot of clues, with every damn one of them leading back to those musicians," John said, nodding and rubbing his forehead.

"'Turn him to any cause of policy, the Gordian knot of it he will unloose, familiar as his garter,'" Jake said.

Lady Anthea gave him a grateful smile, like she'd been starved for refinement, and for my benefit said, "Shakespeare, *Henry V.*"

"Sue, got any Elvis wisdom for us to give back to them?" John asked, with a laugh.

"I'm torn between 'Devil in Disguise' and 'It's a Sin to Tell a Lie.'"

"Look!" Lady Anthea's hand flew to her pearl choker. She pointed at the sidewalk on the Market Street side of the church.

We turned to see the Potomac Symphony Orchestra musicians streaming out of Hotel Rodney and crossing the side street, led by an unsmiling Cordy Galligan. She and the other violinists held their instruments at their sides. They turned onto Second Avenue in front of the church. At the stone walkway leading up to us and the red doors, those carrying their instruments lifted them.

The sixteen women and two men violinists filed past us, two by two, playing without sheet music. We separated to make way for them.

"That's 'Is This Love' by Bob Marley," John said.

They were followed by the triangle player, Beaut Richards-Tinsman, and I saw she was crying. I looked over my shoulder at John and nodded. She was the one we'd pick off from the group.

* * * *

St. Peter's Church had been founded in 1681 and the building was anything but ostentatious. I couldn't imagine a more fitting place for Nick Knightley's memorial service. Jake's heartfelt eulogy hadn't tried to make a saint of the young man or absolve him of responsibility for his criminal actions. He simply did not deserve to have his life ended the way it had. Without coming out and saying it, he conveyed his belief that Nick's death was as significant as Maestro Nielsen's.

The parole officer had left to return to Washington, DC and would return when the body was released. Lady Anthea and I sat in John's office eating sandwiches. Beaut would be coming at one o'clock to talk to him. Natch, I hoped that included me.

"How was this morning's rehearsal?" I asked. Albert had finally consented to walking to the community center in the subdivision, and she had walked him over and stayed. She was still, understandably, concerned for his safety.

"They are spent," she said with a laugh. "Well and truly knackered." She took a sip of lemonade and dabbed the corner of her mouth with the paper napkin. "Are you sure Nick Knightley didn't kill Georg Nielsen? If he had the ability to put ransomware on a computer, could he have known how to make it look like he was not in Lewes when he was?" John shook his head. "But Bess denies calling him," she went on.

"He was definitely in DC. He answered the call. And remember he was with Granger until around nine o'clock."

"The man who killed Nick was holding my head under water," I said. "The preliminary autopsy report shows that Nielsen was held under water. One killer. I can't leave it alone or take the easy way out, any more than someone learning or performing music can take the easiest route."

"I agree with you," John said.

I polished off my sandwich and tossed the wrapping into the circular file beside John's desk. "I hope Beaut can tell us if there was any connection between the two victims. Cordy says she doesn't know how Nielsen got her composition. We know that her computer was infected with ransomware, and that was what Nick was in prison for."

John pulled his chair closer to his desk and began typing on his keyboard. "Seems too much of a coincidence."

"That would mean that Georg Nielsen and Nick Knightley knew each other, or had come in contact with one another," Lady Anthea said. "I don't see how that could be. Nielsen lived in London when he wasn't in Denmark."

"Remember Bess said that Roman had spent hours trying to unlock Cordy's computer but couldn't—but maybe he did! He could have gotten the identity of her hacker!" I said, getting more and more excited. "Or *he* could have stolen the score off it."

"Why in the world would Roman Harper risk his reputation and his family's well-being on something so sordid and unnecessary?" Lady Anthea asked.

John said, "So that Sue won't accuse me of jumping to conclusions, I'll email Jake to see if he knows if Cordy Galligan was one of Knightley's victims."

The intercom on his phone squawked. "Chief?" The receptionist sounded tentative. "You have guests?" It was a statement, but she'd made it sound like a question.

We three looked out into the lobby. Beaut was accompanied by Cordy Galligan, Bess Harper and Margo Bardot. Beaut was wearing jeans and a sweatshirt that read, *GOING FOR BAROQUE*. Bess wore another expensive pantsuit and Margo was dressed for success. Cordy was again dressed in black, head to toe.

"We're going to need the interrogation room."

He met them and led them down the hallway, motioning for Officer Statler to join them. Before the quartet reached the door, Beaut jabbed a finger at Cordy and said, "I heard how you talked to Nick. You were dismissive, disrespectful, mean, and condescending to him."

Margo countered, "And I saw *him* get mad at *her*." As usual, coming to Cordy's defense.

"Do you realize what someone with skills like Nick would do if he got mad at someone?" Bess asked. "It would not be pretty."

"Typical!" Beaut snarled.

Officer Statler had made her way through the crowd of six women, four of them angry, and John. Lady Anthea and I had hung back listening, because if people see you standing right there it's not eavesdropping. I reached for her elbow and winked.

John motioned for Officer Statler to go into the interrogation room, then held up a hand to everyone else. "Ms. Richards-Tinsman, go ahead. The rest of you I'll be happy to talk to later."

I nudged Lady Anthea forward. When she looked at me, I nodded to the much-used-of-late interrogation room. Then I yelled, "Well, I never! Ladies, let's go!" As I dramatically swung around to leave I saw I was getting a confused look from John. He must have caught on, because when we got out onto the walkway Lady Anthea wasn't with us. He had let her stay. I looked at Cordy, Bess and Margo. "Where to?" Without giving them time to respond, I asked, "Cordy, want to pay Marin a visit at Buckingham's?"

"Yes!" she said. "Let's do."

"My car is over here," I said, pointing to the left.

"Mine's there," Bess said. She pointed to a handicapped spot. I pressed my lips together to keep from telling her what I thought of that. Why was I surprised? It was completely in character.

Margo motioned for Cordy to join them, but when I looked at her, too, she followed me to the Jeep. I wasn't sure how I'd managed it, but Cordy rode with me, the other two followed in Bess's BMW and we drove up Savannah Road.

"For what it's worth, I think *Sonata by the Sea* is beautiful and moving," I said, trying to make conversation.

"It's *Symphony by the Sea*, not sonata, which is written for a piano alone, or one other instrument and the piano. My work was written for a full orchestra. Baroque sonatas were somewhat different but today—and obviously my piece is contemporary—that is the difference between a symphony and a sonata."

Ordinarily, my immediate reaction to being schooled in such a patronizing manner would have been to wish she was in Bess's car. But two murders had been committed in my town and I wanted answers more than I wanted to put her in her place. "Gotcha."

I drove on through town before trying again to start a conversation. "My Schnauzer, Abby has befriended Marin Alsop." By that I meant my dog had been bossing hers around all week.

I thought about how she'd seemed so attached to the dog on Monday, but she hadn't even asked about her since, nor had she visited. "You know, you're welcome to drop by anytime to spend time with her," I offered.

She nodded but didn't speak. Suddenly puzzle pieces started moving into place in my mind's eye. Starting with the last-minute boarding request, moving on to Bess's daughter's sneezing fit when we went to their house after the press conference. What was her name? Sophie. That was it. The girl obviously had allergies, but we hadn't brought a dog with us. "Had you and Marin planned to stay at Bess's house?"

"Yes," she said through gritted teeth. "Marin Alsop and I were coming on Sunday."

"How bad are Sophie's allergies?"

"Very." Abby's post-grooming kerchief had been in my pocket, so that would be very, very severe. Since Marin Alsop was being boarded, why wasn't Cordy staying with Bess rather than at Hotel Rodney? The house was certainly large enough, even with Sophie there. If Cordy's current sullen attitude was any indication, it was because she was pouting.

"I hope there were no hard feelings about you staying at the hotel instead of with Bess," I said. I mentally patted myself on the back for putting all this together, but since it had nothing to do with the case, I needed to move on to something that did. "Georg Nielsen wasn't in the States when he started passing your work off as his, was he?"

"No, and as I already said, I don't know how he got it."

"Was it on your computer?" I asked.

"Yes, and my computer was hacked, but I had a handwritten copy. Look, if you're implying he hacked my computer, forget it. He knew as much about computers as that duke knows about conducting."

"That little, huh?"

"Maybe less. He didn't even know how to text."

I laughed and the mood in the Jeep was a little lighter. "Is the final movement the most difficult?" I asked, making the right into Villages of Five Points. Bess and Margo were still behind us.

"No, not really. Why do you ask?"

"I got the impression it was from listening to you rehearse."

I pulled into a parking spot and opened the door. Cordy hadn't moved and she looked straight ahead. I got out and stood by the open door, waiting. Finally, she spoke. "I never finished composing the final movement. I started it but I didn't get very far. Maestro Nielsen changed it and wrote his own final movement. It's new to me, that's why I play it with such hesitancy."

"Which is why the rest of the orchestra stumbles over it," I offered.

She smiled, like she was rewarding me for at least getting that right.

"Do they know that you wrote *Symphony by the Sea*?" I asked.

"No, I should tell them. I will, soon."

Bess and Margo parked in the spot next to the Jeep's passenger side. The four of us went into the Pet Palace.

Shelby was behind the desk. I breathed in the calm, the elegance and the dog smells that I loved so much. I told her that Cordy wanted to visit Marin for a bit. My first stop was my office to pet Abby. I returned to the reception desk and she followed, walking close to my leg. Buckingham's usually unflappable assistant manager looked down the hallway for the second time in the minutes that I'd been back.

Abby kept an eye on me because of the short-nosed interloper. I leaned over and twirled one of her ears. "Are you my guard dog?" Little did she know that I was just as anxious for the symphony orchestra to leave Lewes as she was, though for a different reason.

"Marin Alsop is playing outside. I'll call someone to take you to see her," Shelby said, reaching for the phone to use the intercom.

Bess plopped her handbag down and began rummaging through it. "Cordy, I want to take care of this for you since it's all my fault your dog has to be here." She said it like the Pekingese was in San Quentin, rather than a luxurious, if I do say so myself, pet spa. She pulled out a matching green leather wallet and from that extracted a black American Express credit card.

Shelby took it and said, "We don't have her final bill yet for boarding and day camp. We're giving her complimentary brushing and cleaning of the skin folds on her face every day, and extra TLC sessions to help with her stress. How about I charge five hundred for now?"

Bess gulped. "That's fine." She was definitely not a dog person, otherwise she would have been amazed at the free grooming services we were including. I expected a different reaction from Cordy, who stood there silent except for an appreciative whisper and smile.

As Shelby processed the charge, one of the nannies came up. "Which playground is Marin in?" she asked.

"The smaller one," said the middle-aged woman, who looked like she could be a British nanny.

"Can you escort them to see her?" Shelby motioned to Cordy. "This is Cordy Galligan, her mom."

I saw Bess and Margo exchange eye rolls.

"Sue, could I speak with you in private?" Margo said.

"Sure." I motioned for her to come back to my office.

She sat on the sofa and I sat behind my desk. Her gaze drifted to the window over my shoulder. If anyone other than Margo Bardot was sitting across from me I would have thought she was getting up her nerve to speak, but it was her.

Finally, she said, "I have a confession to make. I told Nick Knightley how valuable a music score is, especially an original, unperformed composition. I fear that may have prompted him to hack Cordy's computer and steal it." So Cordy had told them she was the composer of the new piece.

"The timeline's wrong. He wasn't working for the PSO when her computer was hacked," I reminded her. Surely she knew that.

"No," she said. "You're right." She was, for once, speaking at normal speed. "You see, if he had the composition, my comment might have given him the idea to sell it to Maestro Nielsen when he came to meet with us." Just like that she'd been caught in one lie and had flipped to another. Or was the last part true? No, it couldn't be. Nielsen had sent the score to the librarian before he arrived.

"Why would he pick Georg Nielsen to sell it to? Did he know him?" I doubted their paths would have crossed. One was a Danish composer and the other an American prison inmate. That seemed as likely as there being a single word of truth in what she was saying. Still, she could change my mind if she told me something, anything, linking the two victims.

She shrugged. "I don't know." Then she stood and walked out. I followed her, and when I walked behind Shelby, she craned around to peer down the hallway.

We made eye contact and I gave her a *what's up* look.

Tell you later, she mouthed.

I kept walking and took Margo to the playground where the others were.

Cordy was sitting cross-legged on the grass, petting her dog. There was a wooden park bench against each of the three high fences. Bess sat on the one directly across from the door. Her large handbag was on the ground by her feet. Four dogs gamboled across the blue climbing bridge. Some of them stopped to look at us by peeking between the white foamy waves painted on its top edge. I joined the nanny who leaned against the yellow wooden chair with *LIFEGUARD* stenciled on the back. "Gorgeous weather," she said.

I agreed and closed my eyes and breathed it in.

Marin ran to my employee and the woman reached down to stroke her back. Then she ran over the bridge. She was having a good time. Cordy stared at her in disbelief. "I've never seen her this active," she said.

Hearing Cordy's voice, Marin ran down from the bridge and ran a lap around the playground, slowing down briefly to sniff inside Bess's buttery leather handbag. I went over to sit next to Bess. "How did you know how to find Albert on Monday?" I asked. It was a question that had been bothering me.

She turned to face me and said, "My husband found him. He found your address online and we drove over. The duke came out when he saw us in your driveway."

Marin Alsop was back and had her nose in Bess's handbag again. Cordy walked over to pull her out but Marin ran back to the bridge, this time running under it. When she came out the other side, Cordy was waiting to pick her up. She nuzzled the dog's neck and held her for a moment before putting her back on the ground. "I guess we had better get back. I'd like to nap before our nighttime rehearsal."

I thanked the nanny and walked them out, then went back to Shelby. I told her all about Nick Knightley's memorial service and how tired the musicians were getting. She high-fived me. "Looks like our plan is working. I hope the triangle player gives up some good dirt."

My cell phone pinged and I pulled it from my pocket. "It's a text from Lady Anthea. She's in John's office looking at the music they got off the USB drive." I wrote back, *See if the last movement is on there.*

"She didn't say what she learned from the triangle player?" Shelby asked.

"Look what someone left." The nanny was back, holding a green leather wallet. "I found it on the ground under the bridge."

"That belongs to Bess Harper," I said. "Marin Alsop must have taken it out of her handbag." Abby got up from her bed and walked up to the nanny. She sniffed and went back in my office, satisfied the little home-wrecker wasn't around me.

Chapter 35

It was time for what we called afternoon tea, though it was really afternoon treat. The nanny went back to the playground with fresh water and a box of gluten-free goodies. I texted Lady Anthea that I would pick her up. "And then we'll take this back to its rightful owner," I said to Shelby. The lobby was empty so we could talk for a few minutes before I left again. "Where's Albert?"

"With Mason and Joey," she whispered. "He's been here since Lady Anthea walked back with him from the morning rehearsal."

"Is that why you keep looking back there?"

"Yeah." I waited because I knew there was more on her mind. "He's still saying "if" you go back with them to Frithsden."

"I've always wanted to see their home! Want to go, too? Maybe we can all—"

"No, just you."

"John and I have never taken a trip farther than Cape May—"
She interrupted again. "Definitely not with John."

"Huh? Wait, is this about Lady Anthea's matchmaking? Because she knows I'm not interested." I rummaged through my tote for my sunglasses.

"First, your shades are on your head. Next, if she didn't set him straight, you would think seeing John and you together last night would have," she said, checking the hallway again to be sure he didn't sneak up on us.

"Even if John wasn't in the picture, Albert would hardly be a candidate," I said. "This was just something she wanted. I doubt he thinks of me as anything other than his sister's friend."

"And a good businesswoman? Definitely that."

"Has he said anything else about Buckingham's finances? Did you tell him he could meet with our accountant?"

She shook her massive amount of red hair. "No-o-o-o. All of a sudden he stopped wanting to talk about it."

"Wait, what did you do?"

"Joey may have used a lot of bookkeeping words that were over his head," she said, with an evil laugh that made me wish I had been there to witness it.

"That made him drop it? Good. Lady Anthea is the one who has the right to go over our books. She's the one our *pet-ronage* is with."

"But Frithsden is their family home, so that might be a gray area." As she spoke she pointed to the photos of the buildings, rooms and gardens that lined our walls. Our contract gave us the right to use these images and, she was correct, they were images of the home they owned together.

"You all have talked about this a lot, haven't you?" I asked.

"Yeah."

I rubbed the back of my neck. "I've spent my whole life avoiding legal questions like that. And you and Jeffrey moved here for the same reason. How did this happen?"

"I don't know, but we didn't want you blindsided," she said.

"I'm sorry you have been worried about this all week. I didn't know. You said he dropped it? Good!"

"Don't worry about us. Do what's best for you. I know he's an idiot, but just think, you would be a..." She looked around the corner and jumped. "Mason!"

"He said if you married him he'd shut down Buckingham's," Mason said, from the end of the desk.

"*He* would? This is what passes for good marriage material?!" I shook my head. I had just heard the double doors open and I knew I needed to stop talking, and definitely stop yelling. "And people don't understand why I'm not interested in ever getting married!"

"I gave Lady Anthea a ride back," John said.

She stood behind him. No one spoke.

I wanted to leave to return Bess Harper's wallet to her before the drama, and the duke being on the premises, could give me a headache. "Shelby, do any dogs need a ride home?" I could take the Prius if anyone got dropped off this early. It wasn't quite four o'clock.

"Not yet," she called.

I told Lady Anthea where I was going and asked if she wanted to join me.

"Splendid," she said.

John got a phone call and moved to stand next to the door to take it. Though I touched his arm on the way out, he wouldn't look at me.

Once we were outside she continued. "I'm afraid there's not much to relay from the interview with Beaut Richards-Tinsman. She wanted assurance that Mr. Knightley's murder was being investigated."

"Like it might not be because he had a prison record?" I asked.

She nodded. "Meeting John put her mind at ease. She also said that Nick would never kill anyone because he wasn't the violent type."

John walked to the squad car, again without speaking.

Lady Anthea looked back at the Pet Palace door. "Albert is still there with Mason and Joey?"

I nodded and got behind the wheel.

"You know," she began, "not everyone is as brave as you and the copper."

"The copper?" I laughed. "I think you're brave. To shoulder your responsibilities with grace the way you do requires courage, but what brought this up?"

"I told Albert to stay here today. I didn't think it was a good idea for him to be alone with a killer on the loose. Especially since John says these murders were of a particularly brutal nature."

"I get it—safety in numbers—but why would he be in danger? He didn't see the killer. Only Bernice and Robber saw him. I mean, other than the driver of the blue car," I said.

"And Nick Knightley," she reminded me. "My brother feels that he's not safe. Since I brought him to Lewes, I'm responsible."

I smiled but I was back on that beach. "I remember how Nick looked at his about-to-be killer. He knew him, and I think he trusted him."

"That makes what Beaut said all the more poignant," she said. "She talked about how happy Nick was to have the job with the PSO; so happy that he would never go back to his old life. She said she tried to warn him about how narcissistic and ruthless people could be, but he wouldn't hear of it."

"Who was she talking about?" I was already reaching for the dashboard to place the call.

"She didn't say. Maybe everyone?" Lady Anthea answered.

"Narcissistic sounds like she had someone in mind." My call went through. "John?"

"Yes," he barked. Was he pouting?

"Can you get someone to Hotel Rodney? I think Beaut is in danger."

"It's too late. She's been murdered. I'm bringing Cordy Galligan in for protective custody, which she is not going to be happy about. Get back to Buckingham's and stay there." He hung up.

We were at the end of Savannah Road at the Lewes Beach parking lot. I looked to my left for a parking spot on Bayview Avenue and saw one waiting for me. "I'll return her wallet and be right back," I said, jumping out of the Jeep.

I knocked on the door and waited. Bess's white BMW was parked in their parking spot, but since most of the living was done on the upper levels it would take a moment for her to come to the door. Someone was walking around in the house but it didn't sound like the footsteps were getting any closer. I turned around to check on Lady Anthea. She clutched her pearls and stared straight ahead. Then a noise drew her attention. She got out of the car and held my phone up. "Answer it," I called out.

The cavorting dolphin was next to my foot, giving me an idea. Hmm.

Lady Anthea walked in front of the Jeep and up the Harpers' driveway, holding my phone out for me. I took it and motioned to the statue with a raised eyebrow. "Remember? The key is underneath it."

"It's John," she said, handing me the phone. She looked down at the dolphin. "Dare we?" she whispered.

"We'll go back to Buckingham's," I promised him, gladly. I pressed the phone against my shoulder. "We can open the door and throw it in," I whispered. "We've done worse."

"Where are you?" John yelled.

Roman Harper opened the glass storm door. His right hand was on the frame. I hung up. After a jolt I hoped he hadn't noticed, I said, "Bess left this." Why hadn't I outed Marin Alsop for her petty theft? I had no idea why that seemed important. It wasn't. "Uh, here it is."

I shoved the green leather wallet at him, locking eyes. His expression slackened and then hardened. One second I was looking at a vase, the next a profile of two old people. Lady Anthea realized something was very wrong and instinctively wanted to get to safety. I motioned for her to walk in front of me. Roman Harper needed to see that I wasn't running. That *was* important to me.

Chapter 36

"Roman Harper killed Nick Knightley and Georg Nielsen and probably Beaut Richards-Tinsman," I said when I got John back on the phone. We turned onto Savannah Road and I looked to my right down Bayview. He was still standing there, holding his door open. He smiled and shrugged before going back inside, speaking to someone. Bess? Sophie?

"Where are you now?"

"Lady Anthea and I are headed back to Buckingham's."

"Why don't you come here? It's closer."

I looked at Lady Anthea and saw the worry for her brother on her face. "I need to be at Buckingham's."

"Will you stay in tonight?" John asked.

"Yes. Sure. Aren't you going to arrest him?"

"On what grounds?"

"I saw his hand! It's him!"

"I need more."

Lady Anthea leaned closer to the dash to speak to John. "How was Beaut murdered?"

"She was shot. Looks like the same gun that was used to kill Knightley. They're processing the crime scene. All hell's breaking loose down here with these musicians. They can't stop fighting long enough to give us anything usable. I'm bringing officers in from other areas to take their statements." He hesitated, then said, "Sue, I need to know I don't have to worry about you."

"I'll stay put. Remember Charles Andrews was a district attorney. Maybe you could deputize him," I said.

He yelled to someone in the background. "Anybody have Charles Andrews's phone number?"

"I'll send it to you. Call him, don't text," I advised.

Chapter 37

When we got back to Buckingham's we had just enough time to tell Shelby, Mason, Joey and Albert about the latest murder before the late-day rush began. Lady Anthea hadn't wanted to bring her brother downstairs out of the grooming suite to hear it, but I had insisted. She looked at me and took a deep breath. "It's time, isn't it?"

"Yes," I said. "He deserves to know everything we know."

When we finished, Lady Anthea made a flapping gesture with her hands. "You three should go home now."

Mason and Joey shook their heads no and Shelby said, "We can't let everyone go, so we all stay until all the dogs are picked up."

"Is no one in this town safe?" Albert said. His eyes were bulging with anger.

"We're safe as houses!" Lady Anthea assured him.

"You weren't here last weekend when the first two murders were committed, so what do you have to worry about?" Joey asked, not angrily, but there was a challenge in his voice I had never heard before.

Rather than answer Joey, Albert turned to me. His face was so close I could see the pores of his pale skin. "Let me rephrase that," Albert spat out his words. "Is anyone safe around you?"

"That's quite enough!" Lady Anthea said.

"The answer is probably not." My unruffled but serious tone seemed to irritate him further and he sputtered.

Lady Anthea huffed in exasperation. "We could do with a bit less honesty."

"Joey, are you all right?" I asked.

He nodded two quick jerks.

"Shelby, do we have any dogs to drop off?"

"It's time to take Robber and Dottie home."

"Mason? Joey? Can you drop them off?" I asked.

Mason said, "We'll drop Dottie off first and then go on to Kate's in Rehoboth Beach, near home." They both bowed to Lady Anthea and I wondered if Albert had seen them do that before.

"Do they know that's not expected?" he yelled.

"Albert, it's just something—" I started.

"It's *sir* to you!"

"What?" I was about to laugh.

"The first time you greeted me you were to have referred to me as *Your Grace*, and sir after that!"

I ignored him and turned to Mason and Joey. "I saw Roman Harper's hands. He killed Georg Nielsen and Nick Knightley and probably Beaut."

"Who cares about them?" Mason yelled. "He tried to kill you!"

"Have they arrested him?" Joey asked, touching Mason's arm.

"John says he needs evidence," I said.

"Well, imagine that," Albert said with sarcasm I didn't know he had the intelligence for. He was getting harder to ignore. His volume had risen high enough for Abby to come out of my office. She looked at me for a sign and I smiled to relax her.

I turned back to Mason and Joey. "I told you about Roman Harper since you'll be going to downtown Lewes near Hotel Rodney when you drop Dayle's Dalmatian off. Be careful and text us when you get home."

Albert pointed to the door and jumped. "Who's that?" he yelled. "He's coming in!"

Shelby was the first one to regain the ability to breathe and speak. "She's here to pick up her dog from day camp!" Then she smiled at the pet parent, Lewes mayor Betsy Rivard, who was approaching the reception desk.

I greeted Betsy, then said to Albert, "Let's go upstairs before you scare anyone."

I had to touch his arm to get his attention as he gawked at Lady Anthea. His sister had joined Shelby behind the desk and was using the intercom to request Betsy's poodle, Paris, be brought out.

She looked at him and said, "This is what is referred to as work."

"Sue, Chief Turner just updated me," Betsy said as she waited. "Oh, are you Albert, Duke of Norwall?"

"At your service," he said.

I introduced them. "You can feel safe in Lewes," Betsy said. "We have one of the best police chiefs in the state. Maybe on the East Coast. He's hardworking, brilliant and well respected in the community." She smiled at me. "And any problems he may have had from being a newcomer, Sue has bridged. She and your sister always get their man." The last she said with a laugh.

A nanny had brought Paris up to us and handed her the leash. Albert was watching his sister, and Betsy used his inattention to waggle her eyebrows at me. With a quick wave to the others she turned and I followed her out. When we were outside I took a deep breath.

"Sue, he is close to making an arrest, isn't he?" She kept her expression lighthearted for the benefit of the pet parents walking by us in increasing numbers, but in spite of her best efforts, I heard panic in her voice.

"Yes, he knows who to arrest, but he feels he needs more solid evidence."

"Are we talking about the same Chief Turner? The fine-looking man you're sleeping with?"

I nodded.

"Haven't you always had the opposite problem with him? He's always labeled some poor citizen a suspect too early!"

"Yeah, he is, let's say, decisive," I said. She interrupted me with a harrumph. I continued, "But he always comes around. My point is, if he says he needs more evidence to arrest Roman Harper, he does."

Betsy choked and leaned over, clutching her waist. I grabbed her shoulders. "Who? Did you just say Roman Harper?"

I nodded.

"The billionaire? Married to socialite Bess Harper? Patron of the arts?"

"One and the same," I said.

"That couple is at the intersection of the wealth of technology and the need for arts funding," she said. "Do you have any idea how much money one creates and how much the other needs? And the PSO chose Lewes, a town of three thousand people, to come to with none other than Maestro Georg Nielsen!"

"I get that you don't want to call bullshit on the cultural establishment, but no one gets away with murder," I said.

Her phone rang and mine pinged and we reached for them. Before I answered mine, I hugged her.

"Sue, stay safe," she said, as she and Paris walked to her car.

"You too," I called after her.

As I walked back inside I looked at my phone and saw a message from John. *Charles Andrews says to comp him a night in a large sleepover suite for So-Long.*

Sure, I texted back.

"Shelby," I whispered. "Call the hostesses scheduled for tonight and tell them not to come. I'll spend the night with the boarders." We have a group of six moms who job-share the overnight hours.

She nodded and picked up her phone to text. "I'll tell Jeffrey to bring me clean clothes." Then she telephoned Taylor Dalton and Laurie Williams.

"Where's Albert?" I asked.

Lady Anthea was inputting So-Long's new credit on the computer and said, "Abby took him upstairs. I think you're going to regret teaching her to use the lift."

"She taught herself, and I already do."

Chapter 38

At seven o'clock we locked the doors and set the alarm. Lady Anthea and Albert chose more comfortable lodgings. Rather, he wanted to leave and she didn't want him to be alone. The Harpers knew where he was staying and so I suggested they spend the night at my home instead of my neighbor's.

Mason and Joey called once to say they were at home safe and sound. An hour later they called again, this time to Shelby's phone.

Shelby listened, then laughed and put them on speaker. "That's not the real reason. You guys are checking in on us. That's so sweet."

"It is the real reason!" Joey said. "We need you two to vote and settle our argument."

"Okay, what is it this time?" I asked.

"How much sock should show?" Mason yelled to the phone.

"Do you even need to wear socks?" I teased.

Shelby's phone buzzed and vibrated. "This is Dana. I'll add her to the call."

"Dana! I'm saved." Joey was laughing so hard he hiccupped.

"How much have you had to drink?" Shelby asked.

Dana talked about the trend of shortening jacket sleeves to show more cuff. Mason had not only heard about it, he had taken a few of his jackets to his tailor. "The important thing is," he said, "and it's *really* important—I forgot what I was about to say."

When we stopped laughing enough to be able to talk again, Dana said, "You can't have both short sleeves and short pants length. That's the important thing."

"Oh, yeah, that's right," Mason agreed.

"Because you would look like you'd had a growth spurt," Dana finished. "Sue, are you still there? You're being really quiet."

Jerry had made the same comment. Obviously, the week was taking its toll. I looked around at the sleepover suites. Each was decorated with a different photograph of Frithsden, along with a pet portrait photograph by Dayle Thomas. Dayle was the mom of Dottie the Dalmatian and the woman Rick Ziegler wanted to marry.

"I wish Lady Anthea could be here listening to this," I answered.

"Her brother is family and he needs her," Shelby said.

We all agreed that was the most important thing.

My phone rang again at eleven o'clock. Shelby was napping on the cot and I had fallen asleep reading *Suffocated by Someone in Suffolk*. Abby and Marin Alsop and our other boarders were asleep, some dreaming and some snoring.

"Hi, John."

"Let me in. I'm downstairs."

I took the stairs down to the lobby, and after keying in the passcode to disarm the system, I opened the front door.

"Let's go to your office," he said. "Here in the lobby we're visible to anyone driving by."

We sat close on the sofa, the long arm of the law over my shoulder. "I'd better not get too comfortable," he said. "Might fall asleep." His ability to go without sleep at this point in breaking a case amazed me. At first it reminded me of a bulldog's tenacity, now I knew it was the focus of a Siberian Husky.

"Would that be so bad?" I asked.

"Yes, it would." I snuggled into his shoulder and he held me tighter. "Talk to me," he said.

"We've felt like we were in the middle of something being orchestrated. Right?"

"Right," he agreed. "When we found out Cordy was driving that car, I thought she was the key to all this. Even if she wasn't the *conductor* she's going to do time. I've spoken to the county prosecutor. She's had all week to come in and tell what she knew and she chose not to."

"Have you found a connection between Georg and Nick?" I felt him shake his head no against the side of my head. "How would Nick know who would buy it from him? Or maybe Roman Harper knew that Nick had it from the ransomware attack, and knew who to sell it to."

"The FBI is looking at Georg's finances for bitcoin transactions," he said.

"You loved making that call, didn't you?"

I found that baritone laugh so soothing.

"Can you trace bitcoin transactions?" I asked.

"The FBI and Treasury can. I really want to find that gun."

"Can't you get a search warrant for their house?"

"No, because I have no evidence against Roman Harper."

"How about where he lives? I think Cordy let him out before she got to a camera and he walked to his house," I said.

"Not strong enough, since she's still saying she didn't pick anyone up."

"Maybe his DNA is in her car?" I suggested.

"I thought of that, but they would just say he had been in the car before. Let's face it, you're my only witness for the attack and the second murder."

Halfway through telling him about my talk with Betsy Rivard, I jerked upright. "I'm sorry."

"Huh?"

"On Tuesday when I talked to Bess Harper on the beach I told her I hadn't seen the man. I know it was Roman's hand, but now my testimony won't be worth much, will it?"

"No," he said, exhaling. "If only I had caught him Sunday morning..." His sentence drifted off.

"If Robber and Bernice couldn't catch him, there was no way you would have been able to," I said.

"Too bad those dogs can't be forced to testify."

"Maybe they can," I said.

Elvis was singing in the background, "'Can't Help Falling in Love.'"

Chapter 39

As John left Buckingham's around midnight, Shelby's husband, Jeffrey, came in. I went back upstairs, and we spent the next hours comparing the many ways dogs can sleep and taking turns napping in the rocking chairs the night nannies use. Lady Anthea, Mason, Joey and Dana texted to check on us again. By six o'clock I felt stupid from lack of sleep, which made me especially susceptible when the ocean called to me.

Since Jeffrey was there with Shelby I decided it was okay to leave. I changed into the running clothes I kept at work and before I knew it I was driving to Roosevelt Inlet. I had gone there rather than Lewes Beach because although sleep deprived, I wasn't a complete idiot. I parked and walked to the waterline to warm up.

During the night I'd listed my many questions, and now it was up to the ocean to give me some answers. Like, why had Roman shot Nick rather than me? Maybe when Nick learned who the recipient of the original composition was he threatened to expose Georg? He and Cordy didn't get along so I doubted he would have done it for her. I imagined the USB drive floating in the water. Roman was the link between Georg and Nick, and that proved it—at least to me. Shutting Nick up and getting that USB drive was more important to Roman than killing me. What had Nick told Beaut? Maybe she wanted the truth about *Symphony by the Sea* to come out? I had guesses for those questions, but there was one question that I didn't even have that for. What motive did Roman have for killing Georg Nielsen?

I looked out across the bay and breathed. I knew this was where I needed to be. It was hard to have limited thoughts when looking at such an expanse of water.

I remembered how John looked running after Robber and Bernice. "If you can't run with the big dogs, stay under the porch," I said to myself. Already feeling better, more confident. Neither were trained as guard dogs, but that day they were.

Since I was jogging south, the bay was to my left and I could see the two lighthouses in the distance ahead. They sat at the entrance to the Atlantic Ocean. I thought about vastness and time. Suddenly, I knew I needed to go back further, earlier. Cordy was to have stayed with Bess for the week, but since she had a dog she was uninvited. The Harpers originally planned to come on Monday but changed their minds.

As I ran I imagined I was Cordy. Angry and frustrated that I hadn't gotten Georg to agree to acknowledge the work was my creation. He couldn't agree to that since his contract as guest conductor depended on an original composition. That's what Margo had said.

Still imagining that I was Cordy, I stomped through the sand, and I see caked sand on my feet. Where do I go? To my car? I'm in front of Bess's house. I'll go there.

I stopped running and took my phone out of my pocket. "John? Can I talk to Cordy this morning?"

"That's up to her. She wants to leave and at this point, she has that right."

"They're not rehearsing this morning, are they?" I asked.

"The mayor has discouraged it," he said.

"Good."

"I think she made that decision after you and she spoke," he said, solemnly. "So, thank you."

I brushed off the comment and asked, "Can you tell Cordy that if she talks to me it could be the difference between being charged with obstruction of justice or conspiracy to commit a crime? Would you let her out to conduct the symphony tonight if this goes well?"

"Define well."

"If she tells the truth."

* * * *

I made a quick call to Buckingham's. Mason and Joey had come in early. Dana was on her way home from school and would be at Buckingham's by the afternoon. Lady Anthea and Albert were in and she wanted to speak to me.

Shelby handed her the phone. "Hi, I'm on my way back for a shower," I said. I told her about my mission to the police station. "Want to go with me?"

"Do I ever!" She sounded more like herself than she had all week. "Can you come here?" I hesitated in answering, and she continued. "Please. Albert has changed his flight. He has friends in Martha's Vineyard who have invited him to stay. They're sending a limo to take him to BWI and he'd like to say goodbye."

"Be right there."

* * * *

"She mixes wildflowers like cow parsley with garden flowers such as tulips, and once I saw her make a floral arrangement with wildflowers and roses," the duke was telling Mason. He beamed with pride and hugged his sister. So he *did* appreciate Lady Anthea's taste and hard work. He did know what a wonderful person she was.

I heard the doors open behind me and turned to see John coming in. I smiled at him before turning back to Albert. "I understand you're leaving us?"

"Uh, yes." He looked over my shoulder at John. "Chief, might I have a word?"

John nodded and the two men walked to the gift shop section of the lobby. I went behind the reception desk and checked the computer screen to see who was in for day camp, boarding, and grooming.

Mason whistled. "Nice." A black limousine parked at our curb. Soon Albert returned and hugged Lady Anthea.

When he picked up his suitcase, I noticed the gold monogrammed crest by the handle. She caught me looking at it and raised an eyebrow. *Still no,* I mouthed.

Albert gave me a quick nod and said, "Well, goodbye." From his grave tone I took it I was supposed to understand something other than, "I'm outta here," though I had no idea what that might be.

"Goodbye," I said.

"I'll walk you out," Lady Anthea said.

They left and John came behind the reception desk. He put his hand on my back and motioned for me to join him in my office.

"What did he want to talk to you about?" I asked.

Shelby, Mason and Joey didn't even try to hide the fact that they were listening in.

"He's ceding the field to me," John said.

"What does that even mean?" I asked.

"He's going to let me have you."

Shelby's laugh came as a shout combined with a snort. Mason and Joey had to hold each other up to get back to the grooming suites.

"He didn't want me?"

"He said it was too dangerous being around you."

Chapter 40

Cordy Galligan's attorney, a fifty-something man in an ill-fitting navy suit, had driven in from Wilmington, Delaware. When John told him about the potential for a lesser charge, he agreed to the interview but warned that he would terminate it before he would let his client incriminate herself.

When Mason heard the lawyer would be there, he insisted I not wear my uniform khakis and button-down shirt with the Buckingham logo. I wore black cotton-and-spandex ankle pants, a black sweater and a bone-colored leather topper. My sandals with four-inch block heels balanced the long jacket—and made John whistle.

Lady Anthea smiled in approval.

"We know your real target is the killer, and that's not my client," the attorney said.

John didn't respond and that seemed to unsettle him. He gave Officer Statler the okay to start the recorder.

"Cordy," I said as I sat down, "when had you originally planned to come to Lewes with Marin Alsop?"

"On Sunday."

"And you planned to spend the week at the Harpers' house?"

"Yes."

"But they planned to spend the weekend in Washington, DC and come on Monday morning, didn't they?"

She nodded.

"When you left Georg Nielsen on the beach, where did you go?"

"To their house. I let myself in. Bess had told me to and that there was a key under the dolphin statue on the front porch." I was happy and a little surprised she hadn't continued with her story about sleeping in her car.

I turned to John. "That's how the sand got on the floor that made Bess think someone had broken in." I turned back to Cordy. "What did you do while you were there?"

"I called Alex Whittle." She bit her lip.

"Mr. Whittle is the orchestra's bus driver," John told the attorney.

"I'm letting him down," she said.

"And you told him what?" I asked, returning to the subject. She was not getting off the hook that easily.

"I think you already know the answer to that. I told him about Georg Nielsen stealing my composition and passing it off as his own," she said.

"What did you do then?" I asked.

"I realized the Harpers were there and so I left. I didn't want to talk to anybody," she said.

"Did you hear someone in the house?" I asked.

She nodded. "That's why I left. I really shouldn't have been there. When Bess found out I had a dog she said I couldn't stay there."

"Even after you boarded your dog at Buckingham's, you stayed at the hotel. Why?"

She shrugged. "Pride, I guess."

I was tempted to offer what I thought was the real reason she didn't want to stay with the Harpers, but her attempts at honesty had been so short-lived that I couldn't trust her. I would share it with those who had earned it. "John, can we talk outside?"

As I got up I looked at the lawyer and smiled. "Are you originally from this area?"

"Nah, Chicago."

John pushed his chair back. Lady Anthea came too, leaving Officer Statler to babysit.

"Roman Harper has such a good memory that he doesn't even need to use speed dial." I turned to Lady Anthea. "Remember when we went to their house on Monday and he picked up his wife's phone to call Ty?"

"Now that you mention it, I do remember!"

"Bess told me she leaves her phone downstairs because it helps her sleep better. I think Roman heard Cordy on the phone and—"

"And he was the one who called Nick Knightley, using his wife's phone," John said, finishing for me. "Bringing him to Lewes. I'm going to recommend she be charged with both obstruction and accessory after the fact. That'll put the burden on her to decide what she did or didn't know and when." He rubbed his forehead and sighed. "But I still don't have enough to arrest Roman Harper."

"Let's go back in," I whispered. As I opened the door, I laughed and said over my shoulder, "Looks like the diurnal tides solved the case." I sat down and went on. "Chief, I think it's only fair that you tell them how you photographed the intertidal zone, using advances in bathymetry. My friends, Bernice and Robber..."

"You have a friend named Robber?" Cordy asked.

"Nickname," I said. She would know who these two besties were if she had paid Marin regular visits. "Anywho, they both recommended an MBES, but Officer Statler here disagreed," I said, pointing to her, which made her look up with a start. "She said it wasn't necessary and guess what? She was right. As usual. The predictions of low and high tides are influenced by many factors, such as the amphidromic systems. Listen to me, I'm just droning on when we *all* know the principal lunar semidiurnal constituent is all that matters. Am I right or am I right?" I had talked faster and faster and now I could take a breath. They all stared. Mouths were open. No one said a word. "So that's how the Lewes police department captured DNA from the footprints leading away from Maestro Nielsen's and Nick Knightley's bodies." I stopped and beamed at John, but I had Cordy in my peripheral vision. Now was the time for her to give up the name. She must not have seen it that way because she was silent as a Basenji.

"Aw, just doin' my job," John said.

Lady Anthea slammed her hands onto the table. "Cordy! This is science!" Which it was, more or less, actually less. "R-e-a-l-l-y!"

I bit my lip to keep from grinning. Her brother was gone and now she could concentrate on sleuthing.

Cordy looked at her attorney. "I can give them the name. I mean, since they already know who it was."

He held up his hand for her to wait. "Chief Turner, can we talk about a deal?"

He nodded. "It's up to the prosecutor but I can certainly recommend it."

"Roman Harper ran to my car!"

Chapter 41

The next half hour was spent listening to Cordy swear that although she let Roman Harper in her car she didn't know about the murder or the attack on Sue. For the recorder she went back over the brief drive from Savannah Road, left past the Dairy Queen onto Cape Henlopen Drive. At the intersection with Kings Highway he had told her to let him out.

"What reason did he give for wanting to get in your car?" John asked.

"He said two dogs were chasing him. I believed him because he was really scared."

"When did you learn the real reason?" John asked.

"When I found out Georg Nielsen was dead! I drove back to the beach and I saw the police cars and that white van driving in. I got out of my car and stood with everyone else on the beach. When I saw that one of the dead men was wearing a tuxedo I put two and two together. I didn't know who the other person was until Monday." She looked at me and said, "Now do you see why I didn't want to stay with them this week?"

The lawyer leaned forward. "Obviously, my client would not have driven her car back to where the police were descending like locusts if she had known the truth."

"I agree," John said, "but you could have told me the truth instead of denying you had anyone in your car."

"She feared for her safety," he said. "And rightly so."

John looked at Cordy. "Do you feel you would be safe conducting the orchestra tonight? It'll be outdoors."

"Yes! I want to," Cordy said.

"I'll have an officer stay with you," he said as he gave the instructions to Officer Statler to make that happen.

"I'd like to see Margo," Cordy said.

John warned her not to tell Maggie or anyone else about what had been discussed in her interview. He walked the attorney out, explaining the next steps in Cordy's legal situation, and Lady Anthea and I waited for him in his office. "Well that's enough to bring him in. And I think I can get a search warrant for his house, too."

Officer Statler was back waiting for her next assignment. "Get the officer surveilling the Harper residence on the line." She walked away and placed a call, then she said, "He's about to call you."

"Sue, what the hell were you talking about? Semidiurnal what?" John asked.

"It means two high tides and two low tides in a day. Most days that's us," I said. "When I found out he wasn't raised near the ocean I figured I could get away with it."

"Would any of it have made sense if we had known those terms?" Lady Anthea asked.

"About all I was saying was that the tide comes in and the tide goes out," I explained. "And a few factors determine the timing."

"And you know how to calculate the times?"

"Hell no. I look at the newspaper." I didn't mention that I had gotten the idea from Joey since it was the trick he'd used on Albert.

John's cell phone rang. As he listened his eyes narrowed and he asked, "Have you seen the wife? Or the daughter?" The answer from the person on the other end made his jaw clench. "Stay in position and keep me updated." He hung up and yelled to an officer at a nearby desk. "Call a meeting."

Lady Anthea and I stood to go.

"What's going on?" I asked.

"Roman Harper hasn't been out of his house since last night. The curtains are drawn. No one has so much as come out onto the balcony. We believe his wife and daughter are in there, too," he said.

"Are you concerned about a hostage situation?" I asked.

"Yeah," he answered. "Is it out of the ordinary for none of the three to be seen?"

Lady Anthea and I shrugged. She said, "Should we ask Margo Bardot to call on Bess?"

John shook his head. "I think we know which side she's on and it's not on the side of the angels, meaning us. I don't want to go in there with a search warrant until I know the situation inside that house."

My hand shot up and they looked at me. "I'm imitating Roman and Ty at the senior drivers' class. Remember what Charles Andrews said when they raised their hands to speak?"

"It doesn't bear repeating," Lady Anthea said.

"I know how we can get Roman to come outside," I said. "I'm going to find out if So-Long is at Buckingham's today. Today is his regular day for a pickup."

"I have the answer to that," Lady Anthea said. "Mr. Andrews telephoned and said So-Long and So-Lo would be, and I quote, sheltering in place today."

"Then he needs to bring him here."

John looked skeptical. "How are you going to talk him into that?"

"Easy. We're giving him the opportunity to be a hero with his new love."

* * * *

There was no time to spare, so I telephoned Charles Andrews from John's office. "Finally!" The guy had his own signature way of answering the phone. "It's about time."

"Huh?"

"I haven't heard from the police, but you'll do. At least if I tell you, it'll get to our young police chief."

To increase my odds of a favorable reply to what I really wanted, I let him go on.

"The thing is, the oboist says he and Beaut, the deceased, had gone to Nectar for lunch. Beaut wanted him to let her make an announcement before their big number. What was it? Oh, yeah, it was something about *The Ocean, Our Original Opus.*"

I heard a woman's voice in the background say, "Isn't that lovely?"

She had no idea.

I was so excited to tell John and Lady Anthea what I'd learned that I almost hung up without asking for his help getting Roman Harper to come out of his house. The look on John's face told me what he thought of the amount of information I was sharing, but I wanted Charles to know both the extent of the danger and the importance of the request.

"I love that guy!" I said when I hung up.

"What's his secret?" John grumbled.

"He gave us proof that Nick Knightley was Cordy's hacker. We've been assuming he was but now we know it. At some point he told Beaut about the symphony, but he used its original title. I think she wanted to tell the truth at the concert tonight."

"Unfortunately, that might have gotten her killed," John said.

"Sue, didn't you say that Cordy was going to tell Bess or Margo that she was the composer of *Symphony by the Sea*?" Lady Anthea asked.

I nodded. "I know she told Margo from something Margo said in my office. What I don't get is why it would matter to anyone other than Cordy or Georg Nielsen?"

"As beloved as Cordy is to her fans, an original composition by Maestro Nielsen would have been much more valuable," Lady Anthea said.

I shook my head at the craziness of that. "They did say that they wanted to use it for friend-raising for their seventieth anniversary next year. And by the way, the Bath Symphony Orchestra is seventy this year."

"That's lovely, dear," she said.

John chuckled and called someone in to type. I told the young officer—I think he was about twelve years old—word for word what Charles Andrews had said.

"Did the oboist tell Beaut that she could speak tonight?" Lady Anthea asked when we were finished.

"He asked Margo," I said.

"Wait, why would she ask the oboist, rather than Cordy?" Lady Anthea asked. "She's the concertmaster, and their leader when they are onstage."

"I'll bring him in," John said. "What did Andrews say about helping out?"

"He agreed!" I said.

"How did you manage that?" Lady Anthea said.

"Now and then there's a fool such as, well, him," I said, paraphrasing Elvis.

"That's one connection made," he said.

"I just thought of another," I said. "Margo tried to rearrange the timeline in lies she told me. She said she'd told Nick how valuable the score was and that led him to hack Cordy's computer, but the hack took place last summer. Nick went to work for the PSO four months ago. Then she said, what was it—something about Nielsen meeting with them. He had the music at that meeting. I have a question for her." I picked up my phone and thumbed, *Was Nick in the meeting you had with Maestro Nielsen?*

We didn't have to wait long. *An assistant librarian? Hardly. But I saw them talking in the hallway.*

"Maestro Nielsen would have sent the music to the PSO librarian, who would have given it to Cordy," Lady Anthea said. "Nick would have seen it then. So we've connected Knightley and Nielsen after the hack occurred and after the sale or whatever it was to Nielsen. And we haven't connected Roman Harper with either."

"I'm not so sure about that. When Bess came to the police station with Beaut, she said something about how Cordy treated Nick, and how she made him angry. Something about someone with his skills didn't like being condescended to," I said.

"But he didn't hack her computer in revenge. The computer attack came before she made the comments."

"I know, but it sounded like Bess knew about the hacking. Her comment made me think she was connecting Nick to the hacking of Cordy's computer."

* * * *

Shelby was rested up and behind the desk. Peace reigned at Buckingham's. Lady Anthea and I were in line at the Dairy Queen. "I think Operation Get Off My Lawn should be taught at law enforcement academies," I said.

The police waited on Bayview Avenue in an unmarked car. Officer Statler was keeping us informed on her cell phone and she had chuckled at the plan. We had taken the traditional request that someone get off the property owner's lawn and upped it to something that would really infuriate Roman Harper.

"I see Mr. Andrews and his friend," Officer Statler said. "Looks like the dog wants to stop. Mr. Andrews is pulling him along."

"Yeah, that's my fault. We fed So-Long apple slices. He needs to go to the bathroom," I said. "Badly, but he's got to wait until he gets in front of the Harpers' house."

"He's almost there," she said. "Cloossseerr."

Then there was cheering in the car. "Good dog!"

"The officer is in place," she said. A surfer dude, actually Wayne from the Delaware River and Bay Authority police department, strolled by with a camera attached to his sunglasses. "Sue, can you hear his transmission?"

"Yes," I answered. We sat at one of the picnic tables to enjoy our soft ice cream. Since Operation Get Off My Lawn was my idea I thought we should have been invited to wait in the unmarked car, but I agreed with John that if you're about to arrest a billionaire who has been pushed to the edge you need to operate by the book.

"The balcony door is opening," Wayne whispered into his mic. "Wait for it."

Roman Harper stood on his balcony, pointing at Charles Andrews. "Get off my lawn!" He went back inside, closing the sliding glass doors so hard I heard the bang.

"The wife's checking the door," Wayne reported. "She looks okay. Front door opening."

"Let's go," John said.

"What's happening?" Lady Anthea asked.

"Officer Statler left her phone in the car so I don't know." We got up from the bench and walked to the end of Savannah Road and looked down Bayview. John was handing Roman Harper something, which I knew to be a search warrant. The driving instructor was beaming at Charles Andrews. Her champion had a poop bag and was cleaning up after the true hero of Operation Get Off My Lawn.

Chapter 42

More than a million companies, fifty percent of the nation's publicly traded entities, were incorporated in Delaware due to our business-friendly tax system and state legislature, and ease of incorporation. We have lots of corporate attorneys, but that's not who Roman Harper needed on Friday afternoon. His law firm was one of Washington, DC's largest, but since the crime had been committed in Delaware they had to scramble. They would, they advised Mayor Betsy Rivard, be handling "communications," or what I would call public relations. I had just hung up with her.

John stopped by Buckingham's and we, along with Lady Anthea, stood at the reception desk. Shelby had gone home to catch up on sleep she missed last night and Mason and Joey had so many grooming postponements they left, too. We'd all meet back up at the concert. Even Abby was tired.

"I have bad news," he said.

"Then I don't have to tell you."

"How do you know already? Did Officer Statler call you?"

"I thought only the mayor knew," I said.

"Mayor Rivard? How does she know?" he said. "Wait, what is your bad news?"

I told him about the team of consultants Kirk, Black & Weiss had deployed. "They'll be here around eight o'clock tonight. What's your bad news?"

"We didn't find the gun at Roman Harper's house," he said.

Lady Anthea nervously tapped her pearl necklace. "Sue, I hate to ask, but are you absolutely sure that it was Roman Harper who attacked you? The Harpers are patrons of the arts. They are compared to the Medicis."

"I *am* sure and Cordy identified him as the man who she drove off with." I didn't want to look at John in case there was doubt on his face, too. "How would he know the number for Nick Knightley's burner phone if he didn't know him? And I don't mean know him well enough to recommend him for a job. The purpose of a burner phone for most people who have one is to not be identified or located, so you would only give that number out to certain people. That's one connection between those two."

"Roman could have used his computer skills to get that telephone number. Locating my brother was child's play to him," Lady Anthea said.

I wasn't giving up so easily. "Second, Bess said that a lot of young people in IT think he's a god. Since Nick was a hacker, it makes sense that he would have felt that way about Roman. And he did!"

"Was that how he looked at him on Sunday—like he thought he was his idol?" John asked.

"I meant the disillusionment on his face when Roman shot him," I said. "Lady Anthea, have you spoken with Margo?"

Lady Anthea nodded and looked at her watch. "Now that they have Cordy back, the concert will begin at seven o'clock as planned."

"The sun will set around seven thirty, so they should be playing *Symphony by the Sea* when it does," I said, studying my hands on the desk.

John reached over and lifted my chin and smiled at me. "When is the semidiurnal event?"

"Ha ha," I said.

"The stage has been erected and they were testing the sound system when I drove by," he said. "And I saw Alex Whittle loading their luggage into the bus."

"So they're leaving right after they perform?" I asked.

He nodded and leaned heavily over the desk. "That means we've run out of time to look for Roman's bitcoin transactions. That was a long shot anyway."

"Dana said there are other digital currencies, too," I said, hating being the bearer of bad news. "And the FBI would have had to look into all of them. Want some good news? I might have an idea for how to get Roman to incriminate himself."

"Do I want to hear it?" he asked.

"*Do* you?"

"Nah. It's going to be harder to talk to those musicians after the concert, so I need to go back over the statements concerning Beaut's death in case anything needs clearing up."

"Do people about to be released from prison or recently released ever get a mentor?" I asked.

"There are a few mentoring programs out there, but not enough. Are you wondering if Roman might have been Nick's? That would be so unlikely." He looked out the side window, then back at me. "But since I don't have much else, I'll call Jake and ask if Knightley had a billionaire business magnate for his mentor. I'll ask when and how they met."

"Roman recommended him for the job, so obviously he knew him before he went to work for the PSO," Lady Anthea reminded him. "Think of this as the movements of a symphony. The four parts have been performed in a certain order for two hundred years. Over and over. Margo, Bess and Cordy changed the sequence of events and made a dog's breakfast of it, and we knew the false notes when we heard them."

"When did Cordy try to change history?" John asked.

"When she said she'd never met Georg Nielsen," I reminded him. "The bus!"

They turned to look out Buckingham's front doors. Alex Whittle parked facing our front doors, just as he had on Monday. I didn't like it any more this time. When the pneumatic mechanism that opened the bus's bifold doors gave an exhausted exhale I wanted to say that I was right there with it. "What fresh hell is he bringing us?"

Opening the double doors seemed almost too much for him. Alex Whittle climbed down and came in.

"Chief Turner, I wanted to personally thank you for allowing Cordy Galligan to conduct tonight." John nodded. "I don't know what's going to happen next, but now she'll be called Maestro."

I began to cry.

Chapter 43

We had Cordy's phone number on file and I had texted her an offer to bring Marin Alsop to the concert. She replied right away with a succinct, *Yes*. Her gratitude was obviously of the nonverbal variety.

Now the Pekingese squirmed on Dana's lap in the front row of white, wooden folding chairs. The Lewes Beach sand made keeping her balance a challenge and the dog's excitement added to the precariousness. The chairs were arranged perpendicular to the Bay so that the audience would face west. Charles Andrews sat protectively next to his attractive friend, who had proved to be a real trooper this week.

I was crowded into Shelby's van with dogs and people. The demeanor of the latter was best described as overly solicitous. Word had gotten around the staff and their expressions said, *she could blow any minute*, though I had gotten control of myself right away. Lady Anthea, in the back seat, still looked at me with wariness, the way you would view a piece of recently unearthed dynamite. I had made it so clear that I did not intend to talk about my breakdown that no one wanted to ask me.

There was a knock on the passenger side rear door. "Let me in," Mason said. Joey opened the door and scooted to the middle seat. Once he was inside he bowed to Lady Anthea from a seated position. Then he looked at me. "Why did you start crying when you saw that bus driver?"

Shelby yelled at him from the driver's seat; Lady Anthea yelled over Joey; Joey punched him on the arm. There was only one way to end the pandemonium: I would tell them. "He thought he had lost everything, but he hadn't. He was disheartened by what he learned about the symphony orchestra this week, but music is separate from the people who perform it. He still has the music to love. Now can we please do what we're here to do?"

I leaned forward to be sure Bess's white BMW was still parked in the driveway. It was.

"Here comes the bus," Joey said, looking out the back window.

"You're not going to cry again, are you?" Mason asked.

"Shut up!" Shelby and Joey yelled.

The chairs around Dana were filling up. I saw Jerry and Charlie, followed by Rick and Dayle and Kate Carter. Mayor Rivard milled around shaking hands and smiling. She looked at the Harper house and froze. I followed her gaze.

"Who are they?" Shelby asked, her forehead furrowed. She had been looking in her side mirror at the house. A group of four men and two women in thousand-dollar suits filed out of Roman and Bess's home.

Lady Anthea, Mason and Joey craned in their seats.

"Lawyers," Mason said.

"PR," Joey said.

"I think it's some of each," I said. "I'll text John."

"Are they leaving?" Lady Anthea asked, nervously. "What if Roman Harper goes with them?"

"They're all coming to the concert," Shelby said.

We watched as Bess and Roman came out of the house next. Bess held her head high and Roman had her by the elbow.

"He's hired a lot of firepower when you consider that John never even interviewed him," I said. "Why would he do that if he's not scared?"

"The police searched his house," Shelby said, eyes darting around the growing crowd. "He knows what's coming."

"Shelby, are you okay?" I asked. "If you think Bernice might get hurt, we won't go through with this."

"Of course I'm worried. He shot at the dogs on Sunday. And they're not trained guard dogs!" The image of the man turning and firing wildly at the two dogs, who had no idea what was happening, flashed in front of my eyes and I shook my head. "We have to see it through. He has to be stopped."

I called Kate Carter. "Are you still okay with this?"

She looked around at the van and nodded.

"I'm glad Sophie's not coming. She's so allergic to dogs," Joey said.

"I told Bess that a number of dogs would be here and to keep her inside," I said.

"You softie," Mason kidded. "You didn't want her to see her father humiliated."

"Maybe," I answered.

"Lady Anthea, may I ask you a question?" Mason's tone was reverential and I immediately became suspicious.

"I doubt I can stop you, so by all means, go ahead."

"Where does the triangle rank as a musical instrument vis-à-vis the cowbell?"

She shook her head and we all tried not to laugh but failed.

"Get serious, everybody," Shelby said. "Here's the bus."

The police moved the orange cones that had reserved the parking spots for the PSO and Alex pulled in. The parking lot was behind the chairs and as word spread that the musicians had arrived, people turned to watch. Cordy alighted first, carrying her violin and smiling sweetly. She wore a flowing black dress that skimmed the ground.

"It's her," someone yelled. The wave of joy this created rolled through the music fans, growing as it went. When they realized she would walk down the middle aisle, there was an immediate standing ovation. The oboist was next, carrying his instrument. He nodded and smiled. Everyone applauded. The volume grew until all fifty-one, once fifty-two, musicians walked through. The men wore black pants and black dress shirts. All the women wore either a black dress or a black skirt and top.

The Duke of Norwall was long forgotten.

"Look," Lady Anthea said, "They're wearing black armbands. I wonder if it's for Maestro Nielsen?" I held back from reminding her that his was not the only death they might be mourning. Then she added, "I hope it's also for Nick Knightley and Beaut Richards-Tinsman." I turned to look back at her. "Sue, are you surprised that an old dog has learned a new trick?" She was smiling.

I laughed. "I'm just amazed how you can remember that double name."

"It's not hard when most of your friends have them," she answered.

Roman's team of professionals was sitting in the back row of chairs, on the side nearest us. He and Bess sat in the front row, the two end seats. He leaned out and looked back and one of his henchmen did the same. They smiled at one another. Alex Whittle climbed out of the bus and I got out of the van. We looked at one another and he nodded.

I called Dana. "Are you ready?"

She looked back at the van and nodded. The musicians went to their seats and Cordy took her rightful place behind the conductor's stand. The sun would set behind them. The audience went silent, but Marin could hardly control herself. Dana placed her on the ground and she ran to Cordy, who turned at the barking and the movement. She leaned down and petted her dog and the crowd cheered. Then she motioned for Marin to sit, and the dog did as commanded.

Cordy looked at the oboist and he played that all important and historic A440. The sound of the instruments being tuned only added to the excitement of the audience. Then she tapped her baton, creating music. We listened to the opening of the 1812 Overture. All five of us checked our watches. "Lady Anthea, can you tell yet if the pace they're playing will make this a fifteen-minute piece or more like twenty?"

"Closer to fifteen. And I checked with Andrew on the pace she used during rehearsal, and that was pretty consistent."

After eight minutes I looked at each of them, then I telephoned John. "Let's go," I said to him and to everyone in the van.

We went around to the back and waited. Shelby and I would keep Robber and Bernice calm for the finale of the 1812 Overture. They weren't using cannons or fireworks, but the cymbals would be startling. Lady Anthea and I looked at one another, then we opened the doors.

Chapter 44

The first movement of *Symphony by the Sea* had begun. The sun was setting behind the orchestra. Robber and Bernice could hardly believe their luck. Were they really being allowed to walk off-leash with people around? There had to be a catch. No one was that lucky. "Heel," I said to Robber.

Shelby gave the same command to Bernice and we walked toward the crowd. The dogs' heads stayed next to our left legs. As the music played at its slow tempo, we walked beside the chairs on the end closest to the road and stopped at the midpoint. I snapped my fingers once and said, "Free." And Shelby did the same. Bernice and Robber had the same release cue. The dogs continued to walk toward the stage, sniffing under the chairs at the end of the row. We had hidden kibble on the sand under the seats to ensure the dogs took their time. A few of the people asked us if they could pet our dogs and we nodded yes, trying to not distract from the music, but wanting just enough notice and from just the right person. Bernice and Robber obliged and their heads were stroked and petted as we worked our way up the aisle.

We came to the third row and both dogs stopped and sniffed. That change was enough to make the person seated at the end of the first row turn around. The first movement ended and in that pause, feigning casualness, Roman got up. Bess turned to watch as he walked straight ahead toward the parking lot and Savannah Road. She squeezed her eyes closed. Her brilliant husband was about to make the mistake that would identify him as my attacker and get him caught. He began to run.

Robber and Bernice looked at us for instructions. "Heel," Shelby and I said.

Lady Anthea came up behind us. "Why aren't you letting them chase him?"

"We don't need to," I answered. "You don't see anyone else running from these dogs, do you? He knew to be afraid of them."

Shelby, Lady Anthea and I watched and walked on a diagonal toward the beach parking lot and past the last row of chairs, closer to the excitement at the street.

When it became obvious that Roman was running to the white BMW rather than to his house, one unmarked police car pulled away from the curb and blocked the entrance to Savannah Road from Bayview Avenue. That part was for deniability. John knew the bus driver had disabled the starter. Roman could press the start button all he wanted, but the engine wasn't going to turn over. The doors to the car parked farther down Bayview opened and John got out with two other officers. Officer Statler and two other police officers got out of the car that had been parked on Savannah Road and walked toward the BMW. Her team was there first and she looked at John. Without shifting his gaze to her he gave a quick nod as a go-ahead.

We were close enough to hear her say, "Mr. Harper, get out of the car."

The door to the car opened and in slow motion Roman's feet were on the ground and then his frame emerged. He held the gun, with the suppressor, pointed at Officer Statler. The beat of silence between the second and third movement of *Symphony by the Sea* mocked my stopped heart. Anyone in the audience looking to the left would have seen Officer Statler's back, not that she had a gun pointed at her. From our vantage point I saw her chin jut out; I could attest that she never flinched.

I had Robber by his collar, as did Shelby with Bernice. She looked at me and said, "Should we?"

Before I could answer, John was talking. "Harper, take my car." He held out a ring of keys and shook them. He walked closer. He barked to the officers, "Stand down. Give him an opening."

The three officers took a step back. "More," John continued. Officer Statler and the others took another step back, but Roman still had the gun pointed at her. "See, Roman, there's no need for this." He motioned with a jerk of his head to the car on Savannah Road, still holding the keys in his extended hand. He had placed himself in front of the killer and Roman turned a fraction of an inch so the gun was now aimed at John. "Take the car and drive away." John made it sound tempting and logical. Like, who wouldn't want to do that? I thought about how far and fast a billionaire could run. Roman wasn't convinced.

Lady Anthea had her arm on my back. Shelby moved her hand back and forth over Bernice's collar to let me know that was still an option. But was it? Wouldn't the movement be just enough to make him squeeze the trigger? Someone, at some point, had hooked a leash to Robber's collar. Mason and Joey were behind me with Robber between them.

"If he lives I'll marry him." Had I just said that out loud?

John jangled the keys once more and I realized all this time he had been holding them in his left hand. He was right-handed. And the keys weren't for the car on offer. He was tempting him with the car on Savannah Road, but he had come from the one parked on Bayview. Roman relaxed the hand holding the gun and reached for the keys that meant freedom. The power of the punch John delivered to his body swiveled him one hundred and eighty degrees and now he faced the house. Personally, I don't know a hook from a roundhouse punch, but Roman Harper went down. Out. Cold.

Chapter 45

With the competing beauties of Cordy's music, the pink-and-orange sunset and the lights of the last ferry of the day in the Delaware Bay, the audience could be forgiven for being unaware of the drama unfolding on Bayview Avenue. The suits in the last row were immune to the music because they'd seen Roman's dash across the beach. Now they were arguing. Each wanting the other to go to Roman's aid and everyone giving reasons not to.

"Sue?" Shelby was touching my arm. "What now?"

"We're coming to the end of the third movement," Lady Anthea said, looking at the orchestra.

"Take care of the dogs," I said. I walked to the back row. They seemed relieved to see me, like I was in charge or something—at least initially. Then they saw the look on my face. I wasn't there to get them out of this uncomfortable situation. "Who's a lawyer?"

Not a single person spoke up.

"At least one of you is an attorney," I said.

They looked back and forth at one another sheepishly or accusingly.

Finally, one woman and one man raised their hands. I smiled and they smiled back because they didn't know what I was thinking. *Grow a pair.* "Come with me."

In the pause between the third and fourth movements Cordy turned to face the audience. "The last movement was composed by the late Maestro Georg Nielsen." Then she turned and conducted the Potomac Symphony Orchestra in the finale.

The attorneys stood and followed me to the right side of the stage. *Symphony by the Sea* ended and the applause, bows, standing ovations and more bows began. The musicians began to clap, stomp their feet on the wooden boards of the stage and tap their instruments for Cordy. It was all for Cordy and her masterpiece. I waited with the two attorneys so that she could enjoy every minute of it. Then it was time. I climbed onto the stage and went to her. I took her arm. She nodded and followed me offstage.

"Cordy, they're lawyers. They'll handle your case pro bono."

"What?" they sputtered.

"You'll be charged with the murder of Georg Nielsen," I continued.

"Wait." John had walked up out of the dark and stood behind the lawyers.

I spoke quickly to let him know he hadn't decked a guy for nothing. "Roman Harper killed Nick Knightley and tried to kill me, but you killed Georg Nielsen."

She nodded.

"Don't say a word," one of her attorneys, the woman, said.

"You knew he was dead before anyone else," I said.

"Bess told us at the Pet Palace on Monday," Cordy said.

"But you knew he was dead before that. You had already completed the paperwork for Marin Alsop to stay with us. You filled out the forms online on Sunday. And you wanted an open-ended stay. Why not have her stay until Friday night after the concert? No, you already knew there was a chance the concert would be canceled."

John radioed for Officer Statler or another female officer to join him. He walked around to stand in front of the concertmaster. "Cordy Galligan, I'm arresting you for the murder of Georg Nielsen."

"Could you not handcuff her here?" the other attorney asked.

I couldn't watch, so I reached down to pick up Marin Alsop and walk away. Abby was going to be very unhappy with me.

"You asked me why I never visited her this week," Cordy called to me.

I stopped and walked back. She stretched out her arm to pet her dog's head. "I didn't deserve her. I saw the connection you and your dog had and I knew I didn't deserve her love."

"We'll take good care of her."

Chapter 46

Roman Harper was taken to Beebe Hospital to be checked out, per regulations, since he was unconscious when taken into custody. Two officers were guarding him. Now John stood in the door to my office.

"What made you think of that? We all assumed Harper drowned him by holding him down the way he did you." I honestly luxuriated in that baritone voice.

"I guess it was what Lady Anthea said about the order of the movements. I had been thinking about the order of the notes. It's like creative arithmetic, isn't it? And I thought about the orchestra's warm-up. Those notes aren't in any order and it's really not music. The order is the music. We started making progress once we realized that. It took me a little while to get that there was still one piece out of order. And there was the fact that Roman Harper didn't have a motive to kill Georg Nielsen, but Cordy did."

"Good job," he said.

"You should have believed me when I told you I knew whose hands those were."

"I didn't *not* believe you when you said those were Roman's hands. You have to understand that this was the most important case of my career—no, make that my life—and for most of the week it was circling the drain."

"Because you might not get the new job if it wasn't solved?" I asked.

"Huh? No! Because of what he tried to do to you. And what new job?" He walked in and sat down on the white sofa. He squashed the Elvis pillow flat when he sat on it, but after the day we'd had, I was willing to let that go.

"Lady Anthea saw the letter saying you were being considered for assistant police chief of San Francisco and you were getting an interview."

He laughed and shook his head. Sitting behind my desk, I was out of reach but he stretched his arm out toward me anyway.

"Are you bored here?" I asked.

"You've got to be kidding! This town has had three murder cases—a total of six deaths—since I got here. No, I have not been bored." His phone rang and he answered it. He yelled for the caller to read Roman Harper his rights before he hung up and stood. "I've got to go. Roman Harper wants to talk but his PR firm is trying to keep him quiet."

"Wait," I said. "Are you leaving because of how I've acted this week?"

"What? No! You were processing what happened and I knew you would come back to me when you were ready. Well, I wasn't always certain, but I never gave up hope."

"Then why are you applying for that job?"

"I really need to get to the hospital. I didn't apply for the job. Just trust me on that."

"The letter said your resume was impressive. And why would they say they wanted to interview you for the job if you didn't apply for it?"

"It's embarrassing," he said.

I looked at him, waiting.

"My mother applied for me," he said. "Happy now?"

I stood and walked around the desk. "Yes."

He wrapped his arms around my waist and pulled me in. "I am, too. Want to know why?" Now his lips were next to my ear and he was whispering.

"Why?"

"Because I lived."

If you missed the first book in the

Pet Palace Mystery series,

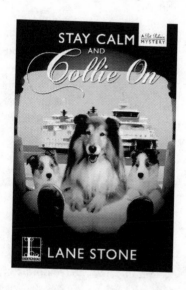

Be sure to check your favorite e-retailer!

Turn the page for a peek at how the Buckingham
Pet Palace began!

Chapter 1

"Sue! Hi!" My customer gave the Buckingham Pet Palace lobby a furtive once-over. "Is *she* here?"

No need to say who *she* was.

I propped my elbows on the reception counter and lowered my voice like I was about to reveal news to her and her alone, secrets people would kill for. "Her flight from Heathrow landed on time. She flew into Dulles. The driver called me from there and then again when they crossed the Bay Bridge." I was happy to indulge her curiosity with minute details; after all, I had worked long and hard to get everyone in Lewes, Delaware talking about Lady Anthea Fitzwalter. The whole town seemed to be looking forward to the first visit of our very own royal personage.

"Good afternoon, Lydia." My head groomer, Mason, joined us, leading a geriatric beagle. He handed our customer the leash, then pivoted to give me a tired, put-upon nod.

"Thanks for fitting us in. I wanted Loopy to look his best for Friday's gala."

Mason turned back to her and managed a weak smile. I telepathically dared him to point out that the beagle looked pretty much the same after a groom as before, the exception being the Union Jack bandana Loopy now wore. Though only in his mid-twenties, Mason was one of the best dog groomers in Delaware. This particular dog had hardly been a challenge, still I complimented him on a job well done. But received no acknowledgment.

"You look tired," she cooed. Bingo! That's what Mason was longing to hear.

"Exhausted. You have no idea." Mason reached a toned and heavily tattooed arm down to give Loopy one final behind-the-ear scratch, then dragged himself away, calling over his shoulder, "I did teeth and glands."

She turned back to me. "Sue, is he okay?"

"He's loving every minute of it." Mason's hangdog expression hadn't fooled me at all. He tells me weekly that he's an artist. On Saturday he told me he was suffering for his art. I slid Lydia's credit card slip across the counter and showed her where to sign. "Both of my groomers are booked solid getting all the dogs ready for the gala." Abby, my standard Schnauzer, still needed to be groomed. It was only Monday, so I wasn't worried. I discreetly tucked the receipt into a cellophane bag along with a gluten-free dog treat in the shape of a blow-dryer.

She patted her shoulder bag. "I have my invitation right here. Engraved, even. Oh, my. Very nice." She paused in her quick sentences. "Might we see Lady Fitzwalter during the week here?"

"Oh, yes. She'll be in and out all week. Drop by anytime for tea." I pointed to the table of Twinings tea and Wedgwood mugs, which we have out every day. Our usual fare of Walkers shortbread had been replaced by the more labor-intensive clotted cream and scones. Of course, the Savannah Road Bake Shop had done the heavy lifting in baking the pastries. I'd purchased the clotted cream from a British specialty grocer in Wilmington. Though Walkers sported the coat of arms and the words, *By Appointment HM the Queen*, showing their Royal Warrant status, I wanted something special for my co-owner's visit.

Our contract allowed Buckingham Pet Palace to use her likeness and her name, but Lady Anthea had gone above and beyond that with her frequent emails, sometimes asking astute business questions, sometimes attaching photos for me to use. I appreciated all she'd done to make the Pet Palace a success and I wanted her to know it.

The front door opened and my afternoon receptionist floated in. Dana would be starting her senior year at Cape Henlopen High School next month. She has the biggest afro in the history of the world. My blond hair is cut short, so balance was maintained in the hair universe.

"Hi, Dana," Lydia and I said at the same time.

"Hey!" She and her hair leaned over to pet Loopy. She's truly beautiful—not pretty, not attractive—but beautiful. She takes advantage of our relative proximity to Manhattan to model part-time. I wondered how many hours she would be able to work at Buckingham's in the fall and how much time she'd spend in New York, beefing up her college fund.

Loopy lay down and rolled over on his back. A blatant appeal for a belly rub from Dana. Lydia shook her head. "None of that, young man. They have a party to put on," she said, giving the leash a slight tug. The dog reluctantly accepted defeat and stood. "See you Friday," she called on their way out.

"Bye. Don't forget to come back any afternoon for tea," I called.

Then I turned to Dana. "Am I ever glad to see you! It's been crazy here."

She came around to join me behind the desk. "And it's only Monday." She looked at the dashboard document on the computer screen. "Looks like we have double the number of dogs in day camp than usual!" She checked to be sure the lobby was empty, then she broke into a little dance. "Yayus!"

I had to laugh. "The schedule is like that all week." I took a deep breath and looked longingly at my office. It's along the back wall, as is the reception desk, but tucked behind a wall. When I was at my desk, I could see and be seen by the staff, but not by pet parents on the other side of the counter. On said desk there was a to-do list I'd pummeled into submission. I rubbed my forehead and tried not to think about the amount of money I'd spent making Lady Anthea Fitzwalter's first visit to Buckingham's a success. Her week-long stay, topped off with the Pet Parent Appreciation Gala, should give us financial stability, assuming any small business could ever have that. With all the new day camp and boarding clients, not to mention grooming appointments, my gamble was paying off.

I turned back to Dana. "We just have to keep our heads above water this week and we'll be fine. I'll be in my office. Yell if you need me."

I made a beeline to my computer to check the status on the few arrangements yet to be finalized. There was an email from Beach Blooms with a photo attached. For the gala, they had initially proposed gardenia topiaries to delineate the space on the beach and gardenia plants for centerpieces, but gardenias were toxic to dogs. What did they have for me this time?

How about yellow orchids and coral roses to mirror the sunset? The photograph was of a sample on the beach at Roosevelt Inlet, at sunset.

Perfect! I wrote back.

All of the gala arrangements had fallen into place just like that. The Event Request Form had been approved almost before the ink was dry. The Noise Amplification Form had been signed overnight by the mayor and city council.

I kicked my sandals off and put my feet up on my desk. I laced my fingers behind my head and sighed. I don't know about you, but when my nails were done and my house was clean, I felt like I could do anything. Only one of these was the case, but that's the feeling I had. Like I could rule the world. Of course, my house was clean. Lady Anthea had asked if she could stay with me. My cottage-style house in a new section of town was cozy but modest, whereas the Inn at Canal Square, in historic downtown Lewes, was old-world elegant. It's very expensive, but each of their seven rooms was decorated with antiques. Who wouldn't prefer that? Lady Anthea, that's who. Her own house had a name, it was Frithsden. Mine did too. It was *house.*

The walls in what we called our Sleepover Suites were decorated with photographs of the estate that she'd provided. There was one for each season. Our customer restroom had framed photos of the Frithsden gardens that looked natural and free, but at the same time planned, a feat only the English could pull off. Those images I'd lifted from the internet. Downton Abbey has nothing on Frithsden. Then there was the revelation, thanks to Wikipedia, that we had been mispronouncing the name of her estate for over a year. It wasn't Fri*th*sden, like we'd been saying, it was Friz-den. For about a month we'd all walked around repeating it, over and over, so we wouldn't slip up when we met Lady Anthea in person. Obviously, she was used to something better than my spare bedroom, but she emailed that if I had a guest room, and that if it wouldn't be too much of an imposition, that'd be A-OK with her. Actually, "brilliant" had been her word. She'd said she would enjoy getting to know me better. Truth be told, it was a lot more convenient for me. My house was in the residential area behind Buckingham's and in easy walking distance.

At five o'clock on the dot, pet parents flooded into the lobby. I could hear Dana checking out day campers. Shelby, my assistant manager, had joined her and was checking in overnight boarders.

The main phone line rang. "Buckingham Pet Palace, this is Sue Patrick."

"This is Kate Carter, Robber's mom," the voice on the other end of the line said. The eyes of her female collie mix were circled with dark brown fur, making her look like she was wearing a mask. Robber was a regular at day camp and always used our door-to-door service. Lewes was a beach town but not everyone here was on vacation. We're happy to pick a dog up from his home. For a fee, of course. I've heard of pet spas in California that use limousines. Show-offs. We're happy with a Honda van painted our signature golf-course green with our logo. "Could you tell me what time she'll be brought home?" Kate asked.

"Henry left at the regular time. He was dropping off four dogs. Would you hold while I check to see where he is now?" I left my office and headed for the reception desk. "Shelby, have you heard from Henry?" Then I noticed she had a phone to her ear.

Shelby had been my first hire. She was forty-five, about five years older than me, and five-foot nothing. With that red hair, she may not be tall, but you wouldn't call her short. She shook her head, no, then put the phone under her chin. "It's Mr. Andrews. So-Long isn't home. He says he absolutely *must* eat at five sharp." Shelby's eyes betrayed just a hint of a roll, nothing the customers in line would notice. Then she pointed to Dana, who was on a call herself.

"Paris isn't home either," Dana stage-whispered, her shiny hair swaying. "I have Mrs. Rivard on the phone."

"I'll call Henry." I pulled my cell phone out of my pocket and speed-dialed his work cell phone. While it rang, I whispered for Dana and Shelby to tell Kate Carter, Charles Andrews, and Betsy Rivard we'd call them back. After a generous number of rings, the call went to voice mail. I knew he'd see the missed call and didn't bother to leave a message. "He's not answering. Maybe he's walking a dog in now."

The three of us took care of the remaining ten clients in line.

"Who was the fourth dog in the van?" I asked.

Shelby searched in her curly hair for her glasses, finally extricating them. "Dottie, that Dalmatian puppy, was with them. We haven't heard from Dayle Thomas. She's the pet photographer, right?" She reached over and dialed the phone.

"Yeah, I'll try Henry's cell again." No answer. Enough of hoping he'd see the missed call. "Call me, Henry!" I told his voice mail. I walked around the counter and looked out the front window. Shelby had reached Dayle Thomas, and I went back to the reception desk to get the latest update.

"Ms. Thomas says Dottie is there. She had just gotten home from her photo shoot when Henry got there."

Dana moved closer to me to whisper, "Where is she?" She motioned to the large photograph of Lady Anthea Fitzwalter seated on what looked like an antique bench, ankles crossed, and flanked by two of her corgis. She was the centerpiece of the painting, but the bottom half of an ornately framed portrait of one of her ancestors could be seen over her shoulders.

"She's at my house." I dialed my van driver again. Nothing. "She's freshening up." Why did I just say that? I hate it. It implies you were something else before. All I know is, it's a phrase you don't want to overthink.

The bay window of our gift shop gave a better view of the side parking lot, empty except for my Jeep and Shelby's Prius.

Shelby raised an eyebrow. "She's probably running up your phone bill, making international phone calls to her idiot brother, the duke." There was a lull with no clients, so Shelby could speak loud enough for me to hear from the store where I was straightening a row of tiara chew toys. We *may* have googled Lady Anthea's brother. We may have done it a lot.

Dana giggled. "That's harsh."

"Can either of you explain to me how he can make the same speech at every charity event and museum opening he goes to, and still not speak in complete sentences?" Shelby taught high school English until she had quit in a blaze of glory. She and her husband, who had been an analyst on Wall Street, visited our ocean one Christmas break and they never went back. She took a job walking dogs and realized she liked their personalities better than those of the children she'd been teaching.

"When Lady Anthea gets here, remember that we know nothing about her brother."

The phone rang and I was back in reception in a flash. Shelby covered the receiver with her palm. "It's chief somebody. He needs to talk to you."

"Huh?" I cocked my head from one side to the other, the way Abby does when she hears something she wants to understand but can't quite make out.

Shelby shrugged her shoulders. She didn't know who it was either.

"Is it something you can handle?"

She looked around to be sure there were no pet parents in the lobby and answered. Then she put the call on speaker. "This is Shelby Ryan. Can I..."

There was a roar over the line. "I AM CHIEF JOHN TURNER OF THE LEWES POLICE DEPARTMENT!" The man took a breath and I could hear dogs barking in the background. I had a visceral reaction to the distress I heard. "Your van was found abandoned in a line of cars leading to the Cape May-Lewes Ferry terminal parking lot. I am two seconds away from having the door forcibly removed."

"No!"

"No!"

"No!"

"No!"

Math's never been my strong suit, but there were three of us and four no's. I glanced up at Dana and Shelby. Their mouths were in O's and they were fixated on something over my right shoulder. Slowly I turned.

"Lady Anthea?" I reached my hand out to shake hers.

This was our first in-person meeting. I knew from her bio that she was about my age. And, like the picture in my head, she wore a knee-length skirt with a blazer. These were blue, accessorized by the Hermès scarf tied around her neck along with sensible pumps. Her eyes swept over the three of us dressed in khaki Bermuda shorts and green tops with Buckingham's logo. We were wearing our polo shirts, our summer uniform. In the fall we'd switch to button-down Oxford shirts. I wasn't prepared for the raised eyebrow, nor the mouth in a hard, straight line.

Whatever. I ran to my office for my handbag—which is really a beach bag—and grabbed the keys on the plastic peg shaped like a dog's tail. I yelled at the phone, "I'm on my way. I'll be there in five." It would take me ten minutes. I motioned for Shelby to disconnect the call. "Shelby, call the DRBA police desk in the ferry terminal. Ask for Wayne. Tell him I'll buy him a drink if he stops this. Dana, keep trying Henry's cell."

As I ran by Anthea, it occurred to me that she might be able to help. What's the use of having a local celebrity if they can't get you and your dogs out of a jam? Without slowing down, I grabbed her arm. "Come with me."

ACKNOWLEDGMENTS

I hope you're enjoying getting to know the Pet Palace Mystery characters as much as I'm enjoying bringing them to you. CHANGING OF THE GUARD DOG called for more research than any of my previous books so I have a lot of people to thank.

First, brainy, talented, and really nice person, Rachelle Roe, Director of Public Relations—NSO & Classical at The John F. Kennedy Center for the Performing Arts, who patiently answered all my questions about the road from someone saying, "Hey, let's perform X this year," to people like us sitting in our seats and hearing X. Thank you!

Second, Michael Globetti of Delaware's Department of Natural Resources and Environmental Control kept me laughing as he answered my questions about the recent sinking (don't worry, it was intentional) of a ferry to add to our artificial reef. I offered to name a character after his dog but he gave that honor to his partner in crime, Delaware's Artificial Reef Program Coordinator, Jeff Tinsman, and his wife, Ruth. In real life, Beaut Richards-Tinsman is a Nova Scotia Duck Toller. Not a musician for a symphony orchestra—yet.

I have so many friends to thank for giving me space when I needed to do nothing but write, and company when I needed to talk: Keeley, Theresa, Terrie, Emily, Joan, Susan W, Susan C, Sue B, Arlene, Margaret B, Margaret Z, Leslie, Elizabeth, Sylvia, Virginia, Lynn, Gail, Danielle, Ginger, Anne, Eugenia, Renee, Barb, Julie and Jackie, and many others. Then there are my super talented critique partners, Linda Ensign and Carolyn Rowland. Love you, guys!

My fellow Delaware River and Bay Lighthouse Foundation board members have been such good sports letting me use their names for characters! Together we've done meaningful work restoring and preserving our Harbor of Refuge Light and had a damn good time doing it.

Tara Gavin and Vida Engstrand at Kensington are great to work with! Thanks for all your support and for *getting* authors.

...Unlike my husband, Larry Korb, who absolutely never knows what I'm talking about when I try to explain plotting or clues or editing. I love him for supporting me anyway!

Stay in touch,
Lane Stone

About the Author

Lane Stone, husband Larry Korb, and the real Abby live in Alexandria, Virginia during the week and Lewes, Delaware on the weekend.

When not writing she's enjoying characteristic baby boomer pursuits: traveling and playing golf. Her volunteer work includes media and communications for the Delaware River & Bay Lighthouse Foundation. She's on Georgia State University's Political Science Department Advisory Board. She serves as Campus Outreach Coordinator for the Alexandria branch of American Association of University Women, and on Northern Virginia Community College's Women's Center External Advisory Board.

Her standard schnauzer, Abby, tweets as TheMenopauseDog. And you can reach Lane at www.LaneStoneBooks.com.

Support

YOUR LOCAL

Pug

LANE STONE

Printed in the United States
by Baker & Taylor Publisher Services